From bump to baby and beyond....

Whether she's expecting or they're adopting,
a special arrival is on its way!

Follow the tears and triumphs as these couples find
their lives blessed with the magic of parenthood.

In April, another baby is on the way...

Don't miss
Rescued: Mother-To-Be
by Trish Wylie

"I don't want your money!"

Anger scorched across her face and she calmed with obvious effort. He could see it in the unclenching fists, the softening of her shoulders, and he bided his time, watching uncertainty war with pride, fury battle vulnerability.

"What *do* you want, then?" he finally prompted, increasingly uncomfortable with standing in this tiny room not knowing what to say or do, clumsy in his efforts to help.

For a moment he wondered if she'd heard him, as Maya's attention remained fixed on Chas, the intensity of maternal love etched on her face taking his breath away.

"I do want something from you. A commitment."

His world tilted as the impact of her demand hit him full-on....

NICOLA MARSH

Inherited: Baby

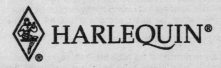

TORONTO • NEW YORK • LONDON
AMSTERDAM • PARIS • SYDNEY • HAMBURG
STOCKHOLM • ATHENS • TOKYO • MILAN • MADRID
PRAGUE • WARSAW • BUDAPEST • AUCKLAND

ISBN-13: 978-0-373-03926-5
ISBN-10:   0-373-03926-3

INHERITED: BABY

First North American Publication 2006.

Copyright © 2006 by Nicola Marsh.

This edition published by arrangement with Harlequin Books S.A.

® and TM are trademarks of the publisher. Trademarks indicated with
® are registered in the United States Patent and Trademark Office, the
Canadian Trade Marks Office and in other countries.

www.eHarlequin.com

Printed in U.S.A.

Nicola Marsh has always had a passion for writing and reading. As a youngster, she devoured books when she should have been sleeping, and later kept a diary, which could be an epic in itself! These days, when she's not enjoying life with her husband and son in her home city of Melbourne, she's at her computer doing her dream job: creating the romances she loves. Visit Nicola's Web site at www.nicolamarsh.com for the latest news of her books.

For Dad, who thinks horses are the best thing on four legs! And thanks to Trish for her horse expertise.

CHAPTER ONE

MAYA EDISON STOOD ramrod straight, oblivious to the huge society crowd that had turned the funeral into a farce. She stared at the casket containing her dead fiancé as it was lowered into the ground, wishing she could cry.

Wishing she could feel something other than the soul-deep weariness that had seeped into her bones around the time she had moved in with Joe Bourke, fallen pregnant with his child and bought his phoney lines about wanting to get married.

Wishing she didn't feel the slightest hint of relief that her nightmare with Joe was over. Or the overwhelming guilt at her role in his death.

Loving Joe had been a rush, a whirlwind romance that had plucked her up and deposited her in the eye of an emotional hurricane, leaving her to pick up the pieces less than two years later.

'You okay?'

She turned at the light touch on her elbow, nodding mechanically, gaining some comfort from the genuine concern in Riley's deep blue eyes.

Riley Bourke, Joe's serious older brother, the only person at this funeral who had lent a helping hand after Joe's death, the only person who seemed to care.

Joe had used to scoff at Riley, labelling him a stodgy, boring old fuddy-duddy when in fact only six years separated them. Unfortunately, Joe's twenty-eight had been going on eighteen, something she'd realised all too late, while Riley's solid dependability had been a godsend since her fiancé's death.

The rest of Joe's friends were hangers-on, party people who hadn't relinquished their hold on her fiancé even after he became a father. They were only here now to get their faces in tomorrow's newspapers.

Joe Bourke, entrepreneur, leading player in Australia's horse racing circles, Melbourne's society darling and all-round nice guy, was dead.

Big news in a city that had fawned over him, laying his life out for all and sundry on a regular basis in the gossip columns. Joe had lapped up the publicity, she'd hated it. Yet another reason why they'd grown apart and something that had ultimately led to this tragic day.

'You don't have to come to the wake. Why don't you take Chas home?'

Riley hadn't relinquished his hold on her elbow, obviously not convinced she was all right.

She'd have to do better than this. For some strange reason, she'd had no compulsion to weep till Riley looked at her with real compassion. Suddenly she wanted to blubber like Chas when he was wet, hungry or teething. Thankfully, her precious son had slept in his pram next to her during the entire funeral, oblivious to the fact he'd lost his daddy before he really knew him.

Not that Joe had shown the slightest bit of interest in getting to know his son over the last fourteen months since Chas had been born.

Mentally chastising herself for paying out on Joe even on the day of his funeral, she managed a weak smile. 'I'd like nothing better than to take Chas home but shouldn't I be at the wake?'

She refrained from adding, Won't people talk?

People had been talking since the minute Joe had met her at the Cup Eve Ball less than two years ago and swept her off her feet, right into his plush South Bank apartment.

'What was one of the richest men in Melbourne doing with a horse strapper? A girl who mucked out stables for a living? A girl who hadn't given up her job despite being cocooned in the dreamy arms of Joe Bourke?'

Oh yeah, people had talked. And talked. And were still talking, a soft tittering sweeping the crowd now that the formalities were over and they looked forward to the elaborate bash Riley had organised at a nearby hotel to celebrate his brother's life in style.

Unfortunately, some of the *talk* she abhorred so much reached her ears just as Riley leant closer to say something.

'Look at her; Joe's barely cold in the ground and she's already moving on to the next rich guy. And Joe's brother, no less! There's a name for girls like her, prostituting themselves to the highest bidder.'

Maya stiffened and turned stricken eyes to Riley, furious at the scathing condemnation tossed so casually and cruelly, mortified that Riley, a man she hardly knew, had to hear it. However, before she could marshal her thoughts on how to respond—which had been to ignore it and walk away whenever anything unsavoury had tarnished her relationship with Joe—Riley slid his arm around her shoulder and placed his free hand on the bar of Chas's pram.

'Let's go,' he said, leaving her little option but to obey as he gently propelled her away from the spiteful woman who'd uttered the slanderous words that still rang in her head.

Unfortunately, people would think her relationship with Joe had been based on money rather than love. People like that, in Joe's social sphere and born with a silver spoon clutched in their fists wouldn't understand how a naïve, trusting young woman could fall so quickly for a smooth charmer.

They wouldn't understand that she'd spent her entire life hoping for a knight in shining armour to sweep her off her feet and give her the fairy tale ending she'd only read about in the few tattered second-hand books she'd owned as a child.

And they'd never understand how a past she'd worked so hard to forget could raise its ugly head and wipe out her son's future.

'It's okay, Riley. You don't have to do this.' She stopped as they neared the cemetery's periphery, grateful for his support but needing time out to process her feelings, to bank her guilt at the part she'd played in Joe's death, and to grieve in peace.

Riley kicked down the brake on Chas's pram and turned to face her, his strong grip on her upper arms feeling way too good. Joe hadn't touched her in a long, long time and she'd craved affection her whole life.

'Do what? Protect my brother's fiancée and my nephew from vile, malicious gossip? Do what any brother would do?'

'You're not my brother.'

The words popped out before she could think and he blinked in surprise—but not before she'd glimpsed a spark of an emotion she couldn't identify. At a guess, it looked like relief.

Not that she could blame him—relieved not to be related to a gullible idiot. Joe had obviously felt the same way, prolonging their engagement, feeding her false promises till he'd finally spilled the truth the night they'd fought for the last time, the night he'd been too tanked to walk a straight line let alone drive.

'No, I'm not your brother, but I'm here for both of you,' he said, glancing at Chas with a tenderness that took her breath away. 'Whatever you need, let me know. I want to help.'

'Thanks,' she said, wishing he'd stop looking at her like some sort of pathetic charity case.

If she'd learned one thing over the years it was to hold her head high. Pride was all she had left.

'You sure you're going to be all right?'

'Positive,' she said, injecting some force into her voice before she broke down completely and wept on

Riley's broad shoulders. 'And I appreciate you taking care of all this.'

She waved a hand towards the dispersing crowd in the distance, relieved that she wouldn't have to deal with their probing stares or harsh censure any longer. Her life with Joe was over and she'd do her best to see that Chas didn't bear the brunt of the stigma she'd had to face.

'No problems. If you need anything…' Riley trailed off, his steady gaze drawn to Chas once again as if he didn't want to let her son out of his sight.

Great. Another Bourke who doubted her mothering skills. Joe had often thrown put-downs her way in his usual joking fashion. Sadly, she'd learned that Joe's 'jokes' were a front for cruel barbs, insults meant to hurt her where she'd feel it most. She'd trusted him enough to tell him about her past—so what had he done? Honed in on her insecurities when their relationship faltered, sticking the knife in and twisting it just for the fun of it.

No, she wouldn't miss Joe. As much as she'd loved him, had idolised him, he was her past. Chas was her future.

Looking down at her sleeping son blowing small air bubbles out of the corner of his mouth, she managed a weak smile, feeling some of the tension of the day ebb away.

'We'll be okay,' she said, tracing Chas's baby-soft cheek with her index finger, overwhelmed by how much she loved this little boy.

And as she gently lifted her slumbering son and placed him in his car seat, and Riley helped load the pram and nappy bag in the back of her four-wheel drive station wagon, she knew they would be okay.

She had no other option.

'Your brother must've been a good man.'

Riley took a sip from his third espresso of the afternoon and stared at Matt Byrne, the lawyer who'd handled his business dealings for the last few years. 'My brother may have been a lot of things but I don't think good was one of them.'

Competitive? Yeah.

Obsessed with winning? Yeah.

Cocky, brash and charming. Definitely.

But good? Uh-uh.

Matt raised an eyebrow. 'By the size of this turnout, I'd say quite a few people would disagree with you.'

Riley followed Matt's gaze, sweeping the crowd which included several TV celebrities, politicians and a few models. Notably absent were members of the racing fraternity—though, considering Joe's growing gambling debts and the number of times Riley had bailed him out, he wasn't surprised.

'Most of this crowd are here for the free food and alcohol,' he said, annoyed at the bitter tone creeping into his voice.

Matt didn't know about Joe's carousing, his penchant for beautiful women, his love of the high life and Riley wanted to keep it that way. The fewer people who knew about Joe's private affairs, the better. It made it less likely that any more gossip would taint Maya and Chas.

Maya... A fleeting image flashed across his mind of the petite blonde dressed in head to toe black, her face hidden by a huge hat, the way her luminous green eyes had stared up at him when that vile woman had implied she was a tart.

He'd been prepared to dislike Joe's fiancée, half-believing the rumours he'd heard about her gold-digging tendencies, and therefore had been staggered by how much he'd wanted to haul her into his arms and comfort her, to block out the cruel whispers and tell her everything would be all right.

A strange reaction considering he hardly knew her. Joe had seen to that.

'What's going on, Riley? You never lose your cool.'

Riley wrenched his attention back to Matt. 'You met Maya, right?'

'Yeah. Gorgeous woman. She must be devastated that Joe's gone. And that poor little kid—'

'Chas will be fine. That's why I flew you down here.'

'I'm still surprised about that. Surely a hotshot like Joe would have his own lawyer to handle the will?'

'I want you to do it,' Riley bit out, knowing Joe hadn't had a lawyer. The last guy who'd been foolish enough to take on that particular responsibility had washed his hands of Joe's dealings quick smart. 'That way, I know everything will be done right.'

'Gee, thanks, mate. Though, by your tone, I'd swear you have as much confidence in my abilities as that woman over there has of making it to the door without falling flat on her face.'

Riley grimaced as a supermodel tottered on incredibly high heels towards the heavy oak doors, either drunk, high or both. Great company his brother had kept.

Making a lightning-quick decision, Riley beckoned Matt towards the huge glass windows overlooking Collins Street. 'Look, I have a feeling Joe's will is going to be messy. Or, more to the point, what he's left behind will be messy.'

Matt's expression didn't change—a true professional, which was why Riley trusted him. 'How so?'

Riley sighed and tugged at the tie knotted at his throat. He hated wearing the things and couldn't wait for the day when stockbrokers took to T-shirts and jeans. As if.

'Call it a hunch, but I don't think Joe managed his money wisely. In fact, I'm not sure he has much left.'

This time Matt couldn't hide his surprise. 'You're kidding? He was reportedly one of Melbourne's richest guys. And you're no pauper. The Bourke name is synonymous with wealth.'

'Yeah, well, I think Joe has been living on his name for a while now.'

While fleecing him as often as possible. Stupidly, Riley had continued to bail out his flake of a brother, hoping he'd change, mature once he became a father. It hadn't happened.

'What about Maya and the child?'

'As far as I know, they should be okay for now. Joe owned the apartment they live in and bought Maya a new car when she had Chas. I assume he paid the bills.' Or more correctly, Riley had given the money he'd shelled out at increasingly frequent intervals over the last six months.

Damn, he should've intervened; he should've made a stand. But then, where would that have left Chas, the little guy who had no say in who his parents were?

'But apart from those assets, you're concerned he won't have money left to provide for Maya and Chas?'

'Exactly.'

Matt paused, an uncomfortable look on his face as if he was searching for the right way to phrase what came next.

'You're really worried about them, aren't you?'

Riley nodded, banishing another image before it could take hold, that of Maya cradling a sleeping Chas in her arms as she put him in the car, a small possessive smile playing around her mouth, a mouth he had no right noticing.

'In that case, let's hope this all turns out for the best. For everyone's sake.'

The astute gleam in Matt's eyes did little to calm Riley's nerves. He had major misgivings about this whole mess: about Joe's will, his helpless nephew and the woman left to raise him.

He needed to know more.

He needed to help.

It was the least he could do after the part he'd played in his brother's death.

CHAPTER TWO

MAYA STEPPED FROM the bath and quickly wrapped her dripping body in a towel from habit. Joe had hated the changes giving birth had wrought on her body: the stretch marks, the new distribution of weight, a changed body shape in general and he'd told her so on a regular basis. She'd learned to cover up in front of him, to hide her shape beneath baggy clothes, all in the effort to feel better about herself.

But then, nothing had stopped Joe's nasty streak when he'd been on a roll and unfortunately, ever since she'd given birth to Chas, he'd been on one continuous 'make Maya pay' quest.

Tying the towel turban-style around her long blonde hair—in desperate need of a trim—she slipped into her favourite pink towelling robe and fuzzy fuchsia Princess slippers. Ironic, considering she couldn't be further from a princess if she tried, but the minute she'd seen the funky slippers she'd had to have them. Spending all day in jodhpurs and grubby T-shirts gave a girl a complex and she often had the urge to buy the most ridiculously feminine items.

Though the baby monitor was silent, she peeped into the nursery, unable to get enough of her gorgeous little boy even when he was sleeping. He looked so peaceful lying on his tummy, bottom in the air, snoring ever-so-softly. A little angel without a care in the world—and she had every intention of seeing it stayed that way. She'd put up with Joe's appalling treatment for the sake of her son. Now that Joe had gone, she would do anything to protect Chas from harm. Anything.

She tiptoed into the room, inhaling the faintest hint of baby powder, her eyes adjusting to the near-darkness broken by a tiny teddy bear night-light, loving every precious moment of being a mum to this little boy. Whether asleep or awake, Chas was the centre of her world and if she thought she'd loved horses, it was nothing to the overwhelming love of motherhood. It frightened her in its intensity yet she was powerless to resist it.

'Ma-ma,' Chas cried out softly, wriggling down further in the cot, thrashing from side to side till he got comfortable again.

She held her breath, not wanting to wake him, desperate for a full night's sleep herself. The funeral had been tougher than she'd imagined and all she wanted to do was have a hot chocolate, fall into bed and pray that she'd sleep. Real rest had eluded her for months now courtesy of the tense, uncomfortable co-existence she'd slipped into with Joe.

Kissing her finger, she gently placed it on Chas's

cheek and tiptoed from the room, heading for the kitchen and the comfort of warm cocoa. However, she barely had time to fill the kettle before there was a soft knock at the door.

No one visited her. Her mum was in a special accommodation home and the people she worked with were just that, work acquaintances. She didn't socialise, she didn't have friends, so who was bothering her at eight-thirty on the night of Joe's funeral?

Almost dead on her feet, she ignored whoever it was and flicked on the kettle, spooning several heaped teaspoons of cocoa into a mug. However, the knock came again, louder this time. Rather than have the unwelcome visitor wake Chas, she padded to the door and opened it a fraction.

'What are you doing here?'

Her response sounded sharper than she intended and Riley stiffened, a tiny frown appearing between his brows.

'I just wanted to make sure you were okay. After today…' He trailed off and for a guy at the top of his field, one of Australia's number one stockbrokers, he appeared uncertain.

Guess she had that effect on the Bourke men. Once the initial spark had faded, Joe had been uncertain of everything where she'd been concerned: uncertain if she was the woman for him, uncertain if she was wife material, uncertain if he wanted anything to do with her and *her* child as he'd insisted on calling Chas.

'I'm fine,' she snapped, the pain of Joe's attitude towards Chas stabbing her anew.

Riley pinned her with a glare, the intensity behind the steady blue-eyed stare making her squirm. What was it about this guy that made her feel helpless? She'd been that way ever since he'd bustled into the apartment a few hours after Joe's death, taking charge of arrangements, snapping orders into his mobile phone, delegating jobs like a king. Introverted in her grief at the time, she'd let him take charge.

He appeared smarter, stronger and bigger than everything around him, capable of handling anything and more. In a way, he intimidated her. He'd intimidated her when they'd first met but then she'd been so ga-ga over Joe that night at the ball she'd barely noticed his serious—though just as cute—older brother.

Cute. What a joke. Nothing about Riley was cute. With his dark hair, piercing blue eyes and tall, athletic frame, striking would be more appropriate. Even sexy, though she couldn't equate the words sexy and Riley in her mind in the same sentence right now.

'You sure about that? You don't sound fine to me.'

He hadn't budged and, by the determined expression on his face, he wouldn't till she convinced him she really was okay.

Sighing, she unchained the door and swung it open. 'I am, but I can see you're not leaving in a hurry so you may as well come in and have a cuppa with me.'

'Not the most gracious of invitations but you're right, I'm not leaving here till I know you're okay.'

'What are you doing for the next twenty years then?' she muttered under her breath.

Thankfully, Riley chose to ignore her sarcastic comment and followed her into the kitchen, his presence dwarfing the tiny chrome and black space.

'What'll you have?'

'Coffee is fine,' he said, grabbing a carton of milk out of the fridge and a clean mug off the sink, looking more at home in the kitchen than Joe ever had.

Stop it! Stop comparing him to Joe.

She blinked, almost surprised at her inner voice chastising her like that. For a girl who'd hardly noticed Riley when they'd first met, she was certainly making up for lost time and making unfavourable comparisons between the brothers to boot!

Joe had been cocky, brash and fun-loving.

Riley was serious, thoughtful and responsible.

Joe had hogged the limelight and adored being the centre of attention.

Riley faded into the background, preferring to take control from the sidelines.

Joe had some hang-up with winning.

By all counts, Riley was a winner; his reputation in the business world spoke for itself.

However, there was one area where the brothers couldn't compare.

Joe had said he loved her, though she'd discovered that wasn't true.

Riley obviously tolerated her for the sake of Chas. She'd seen it after Joe's death and earlier today at the funeral: the curiosity, the censure, the pity.

And she hated it.

He probably thought she was a pathetic basket case but at least he'd been there for her, for Chas, at a time when she'd needed him the most. Which was more than she could say for anyone else in her lifetime, including her mother.

'How did the wake go?' she asked, more out of something to fill the growing silence than any burning need to know.

Riley's lips compressed into a thin line. 'People stayed as long as the finger food and alcohol kept coming. A few blokes retold some of Joe's tall tales. That's about it.'

'Guess I wasn't missed then.' She couldn't keep the irony from her voice though she couldn't fathom the answering flicker of something dark and mysterious in his eyes.

'Joe knew you loved him. He wouldn't have needed to see you schmoozing with his phoney mates to prove that.'

'I guess you're right,' she said, guilt piercing her soul. She could hardly face the truth even in the deepest part of her, too horrified to admit that she hadn't loved Joe.

She had at the start. At least, she'd thought she did. Maybe it had been infatuation, maybe it had been a plain old-fashioned crush. She'd been so naïve, so clueless when it came to men that she'd fallen for the first classy guy to look her way, wanting to believe his smooth lines, wanting to believe that he loved her. For someone who'd never known real love growing up, it had been a heady experience.

'Look, this isn't any of my business but I know you

two had problems and I hope you're not beating yourself up over them. Joe was fun and spontaneous and affectionate but he could also be a selfish brat.'

Maya didn't question how Riley knew about her relationship troubles with Joe. She didn't have to. It hung unspoken in the tense, awkward silence between them and she jumped in relief when the kettle whistled.

'Joe and I didn't see eye to eye on a lot of issues but then I guess that's part of being a couple,' she said, pouring boiling water into the mugs, grateful to concentrate on such a mundane task and not have to see the look of judgement on Riley's face.

Riley was a smart guy and a smart guy would've read between the lines and known the argument he'd overheard the night of Joe's death had only been tip of the iceberg stuff.

A smart guy would've twigged that things had been worse. A *lot* worse.

She'd wanted to explain, to smooth things over with the brother-in-law she never knew but her good intentions had blown up in her face. More to the point, Joe had blown up in her face.

'Why did you come around that night?'

No use glossing over it. Riley had brought up the subject; she may as well finish it.

He shrugged, wrapping his hands around the coffee mug she handed him and staring into the strong black liquid like a wizard looking for answers in a cauldron.

'I hadn't seen Joe in a while. Guess I was worried about him. And you and Chas,' he added as an afterthought.

'But you'd never visited before,' she persisted, driven by some strange need to get Riley to talk, perhaps to give her some answers to Joe's irrational behaviour that night.

'I know, my fault. Business keeps me busy. I'm pretty much chained to my desk or travelling.'

He sipped at his coffee and Maya couldn't decide if he was giving her the brush-off or not.

'Joe never mentioned you much.'

Until he'd gone out with Riley that night, arrived home two hours later reeking of alcohol and spewing forth a torrent of vile accusations that hadn't made sense. She hadn't even known Riley, let alone fancied him.

'Joe and I weren't as close as I would've liked, probably both our faults.' Riley glanced away, a sad expression on his face before his gaze returned to hers, melancholic, uncertain. 'He seemed pretty out of control that night. Was that a one-off?'

She wished. 'Joe wasn't happy. His behaviour the last few months was erratic.'

Riley frowned. 'Erratic?'

'He didn't spend much time here.'

Major understatement. That night had been typical: with Chas screaming in the nursery at Joe's escalating abuse, she'd fired back, taunting Joe, hitting his vulnerable spots, knowing it would enrage him further and he'd do what he always did.

Run.

Not come home for days.

Seek and find comfort wherever he could as long as it wasn't with her.

'Joe didn't seem too stable when we chatted that night and I wondered if his death was purely accidental.'

Maya stiffened, understanding Riley's need to have answers but resenting his inference and the intrusion into her privacy nonetheless.

'There's no doubt in my mind that Joe's car crash was an accident. Joe was too cocky, too full of himself to end his own life.'

Despite her certainty, she would live with the guilt for the rest of her life—that her words had pushed Joe to get behind the wheel of his car when he clearly could barely walk, let alone drive.

She should've stopped him.

But she hadn't.

And it had killed her fiancé, the man who had told her that same night that he'd never had any intention of marrying her, ever, and the humiliating reasons why.

'You must've had a rough time with Joe…' He trailed off, having the grace to look uncomfortable.

'And what are you trying to do? Make me relive the tough stuff just for old times' sake?'

The words slipped out before she could stop them and she could see she'd hit below the belt.

'I'm sorry. I was just trying to say I understand.'

Pity. Stark, obvious pity shone in his eyes and she hated it. She didn't need Riley's pity. She didn't need anything from him.

'Thanks, but I'm fine. You've helped with the funeral and I appreciate it, but now Chas and I would like to be left alone.'

Hot, angry tears threatened her composure. Tears of shame that she'd given him short shrift when he'd been the one person to stand by her the last few days, tears of guilt that a confrontation with Riley could make her cry when she'd been dry-eyed over Joe's death.

Riley took a sip of coffee, his steady regard never leaving her. Even in the face of her rudeness, he didn't flinch or fire back.

'Fine, but Chas is my nephew and I'd like to play a part in his life.'

His calm words embarrassed her, made her feel like a petulant child. 'Why now? You've never shown any interest before.'

Her barb hit home if the faint pink staining his high cheekbones was any indication. However, he still didn't falter or lose his cool and she had a silly urge to push him, to punish him for being so calm in the face of her offensiveness.

'Besides, how do you think you're going to do that? You said business keeps you busy.'

'I can offer you financial support,' he said, draining his coffee and rinsing the mug while she glared at his back, irrationally noting the perfect fit of his designer business shirt stretched across his shoulders.

Money. He was offering money.

She should've known.

The Bourkes had been born with a silver spoon in their well-fed mouths, had never known a day's hunger or the desperate, clawing empty feeling of knowing there was no money to buy food for the next week. The yearning for an ice cream cone or the craving for new shoes so that you could be like the other kids.

Uh-uh, guys like Joe and Riley had no idea what it was like to be poor.

Chas needed love and affection and the presence of a stable male influence in his young life—three things she would've killed for when growing up.

Instead, Riley was offering money. Cold, hard cash to go along with his cold, hard heart. Just like his brother.

'You didn't answer my earlier question. Why the sudden interest in Chas now?'

She kept her voice steady with effort. She couldn't let him see how rattled she was by his offer of money, how cheap it made her feel.

'I want to do everything I can for my nephew. He had Joe in the past but Joe's not here any more.'

Riley glanced away as if he was hiding something but she was too drained to fathom his motives. 'Besides, if I'm not around a lot, you can use the money to buy him things, keep him occupied, raise him the way Joe would've wanted.'

Her eyes narrowed as exhaustion battled with anger, fatigue with confusion. 'Which way is that? Like a Bourke, you mean?'

Rich, pampered, spoiled? Joe had hardly looked at Chas since his birth and, as for Riley marching in here like some do-gooder bestowing benevolence on a charity case, she had news for him.

'Well, yes,' he said, thrusting his hands in his pockets as if reaching for a cheque book there and then.

Suddenly, a sinister thought flashed through her head. What if Riley's newfound interest in Chas was because he wanted to take her precious son away? He had the money, the connections and the power. Perhaps this whole thing tonight was about buying her off, trying to see how she'd react?

Maybe it was her suspicions, the soul-destroying fatigue of the day, the drama of the last week or the simmering guilt about Joe's death but whatever pushed her buttons, she drew back her shoulders and tilted her head up.

'You know what you can do with your financial support?'

He didn't move—more of that annoying pity in his eyes, the final flame to her kindling temper.

'See this?' She tugged on the hem of his soft, expensive cashmere jumper. 'You can take your offer and stuff it up there.'

For a moment, she saw something that didn't look like pity on his face. Maya turned away before she did something even more out of character—like shove him out the door.

'Look, I've made a mess of this—'

'Just go,' she said, stalking from the kitchen, trying to look as dignified as a fluffy pink robe and matching slippers with Princess embroidered in silver spangles would allow.

'Maya, I—'

'Go!'

She stormed into her bedroom, several seconds

passing before the soft click of the front door and the ensuing silence signalled Riley's welcome departure. Sighing, she closed her eyes and sank on to the bed.

She'd had enough of Bourke men to last her a lifetime.

CHAPTER THREE

RILEY STRODE DOWN the long corridor to his office, grunting responses to anyone brave enough to greet him. He refused to make eye contact with his staff, knowing the first unfortunate person to do so would cop an unnecessary barrage.

To say he was in a bad mood was like saying Melbourne was the sports capital of Australia—the understatement of the year.

'Good, you're here,' he said, sending a brief nod at Matt Byrne as he stomped into his office, dropping his briefcase next to his desk and flinging his coat on the back of his leather chair.

'Good morning to you too,' Matt said, sliding the papers he'd been reading into a folder and taking a sip from a take-out coffee cup. 'There's an espresso for you. Though by the look on your face, maybe I should've dumped a ton of sugar into it. You look like you could use a bit of sweetening up.'

Riley ignored him, took a huge comforting swallow of lukewarm coffee and grimaced.

'That bad, huh?'

'Not the coffee; that's fine. It's my disposition that's the problem.'

'Disposition? A big word for this time of the morning.' Matt smiled, his customary wry grin indicating he had all the patience in the world to hear what one of his biggest clients had to say.

Riley genuinely liked Matt, appreciated his wisdom, and he'd used him as a sounding board on several occasions—though he often wondered if the lawyer would be as generous with his time if he wasn't on such a huge retainer. Probably not, but Riley didn't need to think about that right now. He was in a bad enough mood as it was, no use fuelling it.

'Don't push your luck, Byrne.'

Matt's smile broadened but Riley saw the flicker of concern in the other man's eyes. 'I've never seen you like this. Focused on business, yeah. Cool in a crisis, yeah. Level-headed, driven, serious, yeah. Sour face, uh-uh. So what's up?'

I botched up with Maya. Big time.

Even now, twelve hours later, he cringed, wondering how he'd made such a mess of things. Stopping by the apartment had been a spur of the moment impulse and he'd driven around the block three times before deciding a quick pop-in to check on her and Chas wouldn't be inappropriate.

And he'd been damned glad he had when she'd opened the door, huge green eyes standing out in her pale face, eyes ringed by dark circles of fatigue, her lush mouth drooping at the corners. She'd looked so helpless, so exhausted, a woman on the edge.

Not that he'd helped. He'd blundered around, firing questions at her, not articulating half of what he wanted and alienating her in the process. Before he'd really put his foot in it and she'd told him to stick his support up his jumper, booting him out the door faster than he could say, Hear me out.

'Earth to Riley? I said what's up?'

Riley shook his head and stuck a finger between his shirt collar and neck, loosening his tie knot and resisting the urge to rip it off completely.

'I went to see Maya and Chas last night. It didn't go so well.'

'How so?'

'She kicked me out.'

Matt's lips twitched and Riley sent him a frown. As far as he could see, there was nothing remotely funny about the situation.

'Did she have good reason?'

Riley shrugged, clasped his hands behind his head and leaned back in his director's chair.

'I'm concerned about Chas. He's my nephew and I want to make sure he wants for nothing.'

Matt's budding grin broke through. 'Let me guess. You offered her money?'

'Of course. What else could I do? I want to help and she basically told me where I could stick it.'

'How well do you know Maya?'

'Not very well; guess that's part of the problem. I

need to know more about the woman raising my
nephew, to see what kind of mother she is. Ever since
she hooked up with Joe, I've heard the rumours. Gold
digger sinks her claws into rich guy, moves in and gets
pregnant to hang on to him. A part of me believed them.'

'And now?'

An image of Maya's wan face, the fatigue lines
ringing her mouth, the dark circles under her expressive
eyes flashed into his mind, closely followed by the
fierce way she'd bristled at his offer of money.

He hadn't made it as Melbourne's best stockbroker
without being able to read people and, though he'd initially
thought the worst of Maya, he'd bet his portfolio she'd
fallen for his glib brother out of love rather than money.

'She seems genuine enough. Time will tell.'

Matt snapped his fingers. 'Now that's the guy I know.
Give the opposition a bit of leeway, reserve judgement,
then pull the rug out from under them.'

'It's not like that,' Riley said, though logic told him
otherwise.

He didn't trust easily. But Joe's death had given him
a wake up call. He travelled constantly or was chained
to his desk, was most comfortable brokering deals on
the Stock Exchange. He'd never had much time for
family and though he'd loved Joe, he'd taken the easy
option by throwing money at him. Maybe if he'd
listened more, had seen that Joe had real problems, his
brother would still be here.

The least he could do was be a part of Chas's life to
make up for not being there for his father.

'Anyway, how about you tell me what you found out about Joe's will?'

That wiped the smile off Matt's face in record time. 'If you're in a bad mood, what I have to say isn't going to improve it.'

'Just give it to me straight,' Riley said, assuming the worst considering Joe's lousy money skills.

'Your brother has nothing. In fact, he has substantial debts outstanding to several major creditors.' Matt paused and Riley didn't like the quick look-away. For the stand-up, look-you-straight-in-the-eye type of guy Matt was, it looked like worse was to come.

'And?'

'The apartment wasn't his, he has no real estate holdings and there was no provision for Maya or Chas.'

Riley cursed, pinning Matt with a glare. 'You're sure about this?'

'Positive. The only thing Joe owned was the car and that's in Maya's name, thank goodness.'

'Hell.'

Okay, it was worse than he'd thought. A hundred times worse.

He'd always assumed that Joe owned the swank South Bank apartment he'd lived in and had questioned him to make sure. In typical fashion, Joe had laughed off Riley's concerns at the time then begged another few grand to buy a new cot for Chas or a bauble for Maya. The sad thing was he now knew that the money he'd handed over for his nephew's sake had never reached the baby.

'What do you want me to do?' Matt shuffled a few papers into the folio in front of him before handing it across the desk. 'It's all in here.'

'Thanks,' Riley said, taking the folder and tossing it into his in-tray, wishing he could burn the thing rather than see the irrefutable proof of his brother's stupidity and selfishness in black and white. 'You've done a great job—as usual. Why don't you leave it with me for now, let me take a look at everything and I'll get back to you?'

'Sure, no probs.' Matt drained his coffee, lobbed the cup into the bin and held out his hand. 'I'm heading back to Sydney this afternoon so if you need me, ring me.'

'Shall do.' Riley shook hands with Matt and walked him to the door, the epitome of the cool, level-headed businessman everyone thought he was.

However, as soon as the door closed, Riley kicked the nearest object, which happened to be an old wooden hat stand he hated, and wondered how on earth he would break the news to Maya.

If she let him in the door, that was.

Maya gaped at the surly man wearing baggy overalls and waving a clipboard under her nose.

'My orders are right here, lady. All the furniture in this joint is to be repossessed. Today.'

She took a steadying breath and braced herself against the door jamb, wondering if this nightmare would ever end.

'There must be some mistake. My fiancé owns this apartment.'

'Take it up with him,' the guy snarled, propping the clipboard up against the skirting boards and looking over her shoulder as if sizing up the place.

'He's dead,' she said, aiming for calm and hating the slight quiver in her voice.

'Sorry for your loss, lady, but I have my orders. Everything goes. Now.'

When she hesitated, he pushed past her, followed by a slim weasel-like man who darted quick, furtive glances towards her as if she'd clobber him on the way through.

'This is insane!' she shouted, torn between wanting to fight for what was rightfully hers and giving them a hand to cart away every last piece of ugly furniture.

This had been Joe's place and he'd hired a decorator, which showed in every monochromatic line and curve. Stark white and chrome had been the dominant feature of all the furniture, giving the space a cold, sterile feel which she hated.

Not that the stuff had stayed white for long when Chas started cruising the furniture. Maya had done a little internal happy dance every time he'd placed a grubby fingerprint on the frigid environment.

'I'll get my lawyer on to you!' she said, the men ignoring her empty threat as they moved around the lounge room, pointing at various pieces of furniture, sticking numbers on them and ticking off their list.

At that moment Chas let out a bellow from his high chair. 'Ma-ma-ma-ma-ma-ma!'

'Hang on, sweetie,' she said, rushing into the kitchen

in time to be on the receiving end of a rather accurate throw as her angelic son lobbed a glob of cereal at her forehead.

'Damn it,' she said, running a wash-cloth under the tap and dabbing at the mess while Chas sent her a wide toothy grin, echoing, 'Dam-dam-dam-dam.'

'Cheeky boy.'

She swung him up in her arms and nuzzled him, blocking out the sounds of furniture being dragged in the other room and not caring when his sticky fingers clamped on to her neck.

So Joe hadn't owned any of his awful furniture? Big deal. She'd grown up in a house with a saggy old sofa and a few crates for tables, with a bed sporting rusty springs that dug into her back every night for ten years. As long as they had a roof over their heads, she and Chas could make do.

'Miss Edison?'

Her head snapped up as another man stuck his head around the door, a slick type in an ill-fitting suit who seemed at odds with the other two. 'Who are you?'

She wasn't usually so rude but with the Dodgy brothers emptying her house in the next room, her patience was at an all-time low.

'I'm here on behalf of Drake Sams. They own this apartment and would like it vacated. You have a week to comply.'

If she'd gaped at the burly guy repossessing her furniture, her jaw fairly dropped this time around.

'It's all set out here. Have a good day.'

With that, the slime-ball scuttled out the door, leaving

her with a whimpering baby—Chas always tuned in to her moods—and an eviction notice.

She stared at the piece of paper lying on the bench top, the tiny typed words floating in front of her eyes and not making an ounce of sense.

She should've known.

Her life with Joe had been a sham.

His love hadn't been real, his promise to marry her hadn't been real, and now it looked as if the very walls which had housed their false life would vanish like the rest of her dreams.

Suddenly her knees shook and she plopped into the nearest chair before Steptoe and Son pulled it out from under her. Chas chose that moment to set up a hearty wail which pierced her heart as well as her eardrums and she cuddled him close, biting on her bottom lip so hard that she drew blood, determined not to blubber.

Of course, Riley chose that moment to stride into her kitchen, looking like a GQ model in his designer pinstripe suit and slightly ruffled hair. The faintest shadow of stubble on his jaw lent the perfect picture a minor flaw and served more to accentuate his appeal than diminish it.

'What's going on here?'

He crossed the kitchen in three short strides and squatted down next to her, reaching out as if to touch her before thinking better of it and resting his hand on the back of the chair.

At least Chas instantly quietened, hiding his head in the crook of her neck where he could take regular peeps at his uncle from a safe distance.

'What does it look like?' She lifted her head to look him straight in the eye, determined not to let him see her cowering and defeated.

After their confrontation last night, she didn't need whatever he was here to offer, no matter how desperate her situation. 'All our stuff is being taken away.' She clicked her fingers under his nose. 'Oh, and we're being evicted for good measure.'

Rather than expressing shock as she'd expected, Riley shook his head. 'I'd hoped to be the one to break it to you,' he said, sending a pitying glance at Chas that had her palm itching to slap him.

'You knew about this?'

'I just found out and came straight here.'

'Oh.'

Her anger deflated quickly. No use taking her fury out on Riley. He wasn't the one who'd built a life of false promises around her only to tear it all down.

'Is there anything else I should know?' she asked, needing to hear all of it before marshalling her thoughts into some semblance of a plan.

The tiny furrow between Riley's brows deepened. 'Apart from the car, which is yours, Joe didn't own a thing. He had no money, no portfolio and no real estate holdings.'

'Figures,' she said, rueing the day she ever set eyes on Joe Bourke.

Ironically, she'd seen Riley first on that fateful night, drawn to the tall, imposing guy in a tux standing near the band, away from the hullabaloo, watching the rowdy crowd get rowdier. He was impossibly good looking with his dark hair, blue eyes, strong cheekbones and chiselled jaw. However, the thing that had captured her attention was the glass in his hand, containing the same non-alcoholic lemon, lime and bitters drink as hers.

In a crowd of beer-swilling, Scotch-loaded men, he'd stood out like a prize-winning stallion among a bunch of second-string geldings, though she'd quickly banished that imagery from her mind as his gaze had unerringly locked on hers, setting her heart thumping.

She'd looked away quickly, embarrassed to be caught staring, only to find her attention drawn back to him, her cheeks flushing as he'd inclined his head slightly to acknowledge her, a smile playing about his mouth.

And then Joe had appeared, shattering the strangely intimate moment, saying something to Riley before turning to look in her direction.

The rest had been history.

Joe had dazzled her with sexy smiles, fancy words and smooth compliments, stoking her ego, feeding her every bit of affection she'd ever craved and she'd fallen. Hard.

The loaded moment with Riley had faded into oblivion under the onslaught of Joe's seduction and she fell in love for the first time.

For the last time, thanks to the bitter experience. The only guy she would ever truly love in this lifetime was Chas. As if sensing her emotion, he grabbed a fistful of her hair and rubbed it over his face, murmuring to himself contentedly.

'I love you too, sweetie,' she said, kissing his soft, plump cheek before returning her focus to Riley.

'What are you going to do?'

'Darned if I know,' she muttered, wishing she could bury her face in Chas's chubby arms and block out the world till it became a better place to live in.

Riley hesitated, as if searching for the right words and after the way she'd told him to stick his offer of financial support the night before, she wasn't surprised.

'Thankfully, I didn't wear a jumper today. At the risk of being told where to put my offer, I'd like to say that I'm willing to help out in whatever capacity you want,' he said, his wry smile having the strangest effect on her stomach.

It flip-flopped, though that probably had more to do with the fact she hadn't had any breakfast yet in all the confusion. It certainly wasn't a bizarre reaction to the power punch packed by his smile.

She could've apologised for her outburst last night but she didn't want him getting the wrong idea. His idea that he could only offer *financial* support appalled her—still did. However, she had no idea how long she could live off her measly wage and continue to pay her mum's bills at the home so she swallowed her pride and aimed for polite.

'I should be right for now, but thanks. If I need anything, I'll let you know.'

Yeah, like when pigs are allowed to run in the Melbourne Cup.

He nodded, satisfied with her answer, and straightened. 'Good. How long do you have till you move out?'

'A week.'

His frown deepened and she jumped in, pre-empting

an offer for housing or worse, to stay with him. 'But hey, at least I won't have to pay removal costs.'

'Where will you go?'

'I'll find a place,' she said, getting up and swinging Chas on to her right hip, determined not to have this conversation.

She had a load of things to do, including finding a place to live, and wasn't in the mood to face another interrogation, no matter how kind his intentions.

'Uh-huh.'

The dubious look he sent her clearly spoke volumes about his opinion of her house-hunting abilities.

'Look, thanks for dropping by to let me know what's going on. I appreciate it but right now I have to get ready for work.'

'You're going to work today?'

He appeared shocked, obviously finding the thought of her returning to work the day after his brother's funeral appalling. However, before she could jump down his throat, he followed up with, 'I'm sorry about all this.'

He spoke quietly and, though the words had been an afterthought, she didn't doubt his sincerity.

'Thanks,' she said, reaching out and giving his hand a quick squeeze, surprised when he turned his hand over and gripped hers, his warmth infusing her with a powerful strength that had her wanting to hold on for ever and never let go.

She looked down at their intertwined hands and all but yanked her hand out of his, shocked at how right it felt, scared that a man she hardly knew suddenly held more than the faintest attraction for her. And he was Joe's brother!

She was sick. Deranged. Every bit as bad as that woman at the funeral had labelled her and she had to get away from him, fast.

'I really have to rush,' she mumbled, feeling heat surge into her cheeks, knowing she must look like a blushing freak but helpless to do anything about it.

'Ring me if you need me, okay?'

'Yeah.'

She avoided his eyes, turning her back to gain precious seconds to reassemble her wits, silently praying he'd be gone by the time she turned around.

However, as she heard his footsteps recede, it wasn't relief that flooded her body but a strange feeling of loss.

CHAPTER FOUR

FINDING A NEW place to live proved to be the least stressful activity Maya faced all week. Compared with the confrontation with Joe the night he died, his death, the funeral, having almost everything she owned repossessed, being kicked out on the street and Riley's do-gooder ways, moving into the tiny brick terrace house in Flemington was child's play.

Speaking of which, Chas chose this week to cut a new tooth too, ensuring two sleepless nights, constant grizzles and a low grade fever which had her reaching for the thermometer constantly.

One heck of a week.

But thankfully, as it drew to a close, she actually looked forward to the weekend. She should be grieving, pining for the love of her life, but her emotional estrangement from Joe had happened so long ago. The strange feeling of relief which had permeated her grief at the funeral had continued. She didn't miss him. Sad but true.

Shaking her head to clear the gloomy memories, she led Material Girl, her favourite thoroughbred, towards the stalls. The faint sound of a child's cry carried on the brisk morning breeze and she turned her head towards the main house where a nanny looked after Chas along with the Gould children, hoping her darling boy was behaving himself.

In reality, pretty much a single mum from the time of Chas's birth, she hadn't believed her luck when Brett Gould, her boss, had offered a place for Chas alongside his own kids up at the big house. There had been no question of her giving up work: she loved her job too much and Brett said she was the best strapper he had, he'd ever had.

Besides, Material Girl wouldn't run in a straight line unless Maya was around. Seeing as the mare was Brett's number one hope for the Melbourne Cup this year, Maya'd had little choice. He'd offered her a rise, child-care and a huge tip if the horse won the Cup. How could she have refused?

Working had ensured some freedom from Joe and, thankfully, she'd saved enough to place a bond on the place she'd just rented. Her mind refused to contemplate what would've happened if she'd solely depended on Joe; right now, she'd be out on the street.

Or forced to accept Riley's charity—something she definitely didn't want to do. The less time she spent in that guy's presence, the better.

The cry of a toddler came again, louder this time and Maya hurried towards the stalls, hoping to finish up quickly and head to the house. However, with her attention fixed firmly on the second storey lead-light nursery window, she missed her step, her right foot catching in a divot on the track and twisting painfully.

'Darn it!' she muttered, unwittingly yanking on the mare's bridle, who let out an accompanying whinny of disapproval.

'Sorry about that, girl,' she said, shocked at the mind-numbing pain shooting up her calf to her knee as she patted the mare's neck, trying to soothe the horse while tentatively taking weight on her ankle.

'Shi-shkabob!'

Maya stopped dead, leaning on the mare and staring in dismay at her right ankle, which had apparently doubled its size in five seconds flat and was bulging against the worn leather of her boot.

Material Girl turned her head and nuzzled Maya, blowing softly through her giant nostrils, and Maya managed a grimace-like smile.

'You feel my pain, don't you, girl?' She rubbed the mare's nose and the horse whinnied in response.

However, as intuitive as the horse was, it didn't help the sick feeling in Maya's gut that she'd just done serious damage to her ankle. She couldn't think about the repercussions on her job if that were the case.

Thankfully, her workmate Albert, who'd just dismounted in the nearby yard, helped her to a bench and put the mare in her stall.

'You reckon it's broken?' he said, sending a doubtful glance at her ankle and backing away when she shifted her other foot.

'Don't worry, I'm not going to kick you.'

Albert grinned. 'Hey, spend enough time around those stubborn mules and you get used to a few kicks, especially when they're in pain.'

'Firstly, I'm not a mule and neither are Brett's thoroughbreds. And secondly, if you think I'm in pain now, wait till I reach over and clobber you for being so insensitive.'

His grin widened. 'Is that any way to talk to the guy who became a human crutch for you a minute ago? Look at the size of me. You're no lightweight, Eddy. You could've put a serious dent in my chances of riding in the Cup.'

'You're pushing your luck,' she said, grateful for Albert's banter, secretly rapt whenever he called her Eddy. She'd never had a nickname before working at the stables and it gave her a sense of belonging.

However, by the way Albert kept sending furtive glances between her ankle and her face, she knew her pallor and the size of her ankle must have him worried.

His worry had nothing on hers.

'Can you help me take off my boot?'

Albert's smile faded fast. 'It's gonna hurt like the devil.'

'Has to be done,' she said, gritting her teeth against the oncoming onslaught of pain. 'I bet it's just a sprain but I won't know till I take a look.'

'Okay, you asked for it.'

Albert squatted down and gingerly raised her foot to support it on his knee while she closed her eyes at the expected wave of agony that shuddered up her leg.

'You set?'

'Just do it already!' she snapped, turning her head away as Albert eased the boot off her foot.

The jockey had a magic touch. He'd tended horses with bruised fetlocks and strained tendons before. Still, even the gentlest tug on the smooth leather around her ankle sent waves of raw, sickening pain crashing over her, leaving her breathless and nauseous.

As brave as she tried to be, a whimper bubbled up in her throat as she opened her eyes and looked down at her ankle, an ugly, swelling mass double the size of its left counterpart.

'That's some sprain,' Albert said, gently placing her foot on an overturned crate and straightening, dusting off his hands as if his work was done.

'How do you know it's not broken?'

Tears sprang to her eyes as she tried a tentative testing motion, rotating her ankle a minute degree and wincing in frustration.

'You would've passed out when I pulled the boot off if it was broken. You'll live. Now, sit tight and I'll get the doc.'

'Thanks.'

Maya closed her eyes and leaned her head back against the rough-hewn stable wall, wondering when her luck would change.

A few minutes ago she'd been looking forward to her first peaceful weekend in months and now this. She didn't believe in superstition but maybe it was time to start carrying around a four-leaf clover and a rabbit's foot?

The doc, one of Melbourne's elite vets, had a quick look at her ankle and diagnosed a grade two sprain of the lateral ligaments. She knew the treatment, having tended her mum's sprained ankles several times over the years: alcohol and high heels definitely didn't mix.

However, she didn't have time to rest, ice, compress and elevate her ankle. She had a fourteen-month-old child to look after and a Melbourne Cup fancy that wouldn't perform without her strapper. And thanks to Joe's selfishness, she needed Material Girl to win the Cup more than ever, the promised tip a necessity to provide for Chas.

Brett Gould was a generous man and when one of his horses had won two years ago he'd tipped the strapper one hundred thousand dollars. That sort of money would go a long way to securing an education for her son, to give him the kind of start in life she'd never had, and she'd do everything in her power to make that happen for her precious little boy.

'Is there anyone who can give you a hand while you recuperate?' Albert had stuck around through the doc's visit, happily fetching bandages and ice and she marvelled at the huge differences between men.

Joe had been hard-pressed to find a Band-Aid when she'd accidentally sliced her thumb while cooking one night. Yet here was a mate running around like a regular Florence Nightingale. And then there was Riley, ready to jump on his white steed and ride to her rescue if she needed him.

Unfortunately, against every self-preserving instinct she possessed, now might be the time to whistle up that steed.

'Yeah, I can call someone. If you pass me my mobile, I'll give him a ring.'

'Him?'

Albert winked and sent her a cheeky smile. Obviously, he didn't think it poor taste to tease her about a guy a week after her fiancé's funeral.

'Not that it's any of your business, but the guy I'm calling is Joe's brother.'

'The stuffy dude in fancy duds who attended the Spring Racing Carnival with Joe every year?'

Despite the dull throb in her ankle, Maya smiled at Albert's description of Riley. 'He may be a tad serious but Riley's okay.'

'He must be for you to go near another member of the Bourke family.'

'Riley's different. He seems pretty together.'

'Whatever you say, but if the guy mistreats you in any way, he's gonna have to deal with me.'

Albert puffed out his scrawny chest and Maya bit back a grin at the ludicrous image of the pint-sized jockey sparring with six-foot plus of athletic Riley.

Another anomaly in her crazy world: she had no right thinking about Riley's body, about the way his clothes fitted just right to his toned body, about his strong arms, broad shoulders, lean waist and long legs.

Riley Bourke was practically family. In fact, he was family to Chas and she'd better remember it. Given a choice, she would've rather eaten dirt than ask him to step in here. But then, fate had a happy knack of removing her choices one by one and knocking her on her butt in the process.

'Thanks, Albert. You're a good mate.'

To her amazement, the brash jockey blushed to the roots of his spiky sandy hair. 'Yeah, that's me. Here, make your call.'

She took the phone, hoping she was doing the right thing in letting Riley into her life.

Riley parked his sedan in front of a row of derelict buildings and rechecked the address he'd jotted down when Maya had rung him, a sinking feeling deep in his gut telling him he hadn't made a mistake.

She lived here, in this run-down dump of a place with its sagging, rusty front gate, overgrown path, paint peeling and splintering off the front door and cracked bricks the colour of faded prison grey. His nephew deserved a palace and instead, thanks to his brother, Chas had ended up here.

How ironic. If Joe wasn't already dead, he'd want to strangle him.

Stepping from the car and stabbing at the lock button on the remote, he headed up the path, pushing open the flimsy gate hanging on one hinge.

How many knocks could one person take before they folded, emotionally, mentally, physically?

He knew Maya was a survivor. That went without saying, the way she'd handled Joe and their troubles. But surely there was only so much her coping mechanism could handle? And what would happen to Chas if she crumbled?

He needed to step up and fast.

In the grand scheme of things a sprained ankle wasn't

so bad but he'd heard the desperation in her voice when she'd called him, the weariness, the defeat, and it had tugged on his heart-strings. He knew what it must've cost her to call him. She'd made it pretty clear how she felt about his offer to help earlier in the week so reaching out must've irked and he'd have to be damn careful how he trod from here on in.

He knocked on the door, half expecting it to creak open. The ramshackle place had a haunted look about it, as if squatters or ghosts were the only inhabitants silly or desperate enough to take up lodgings within the dreary walls.

'Come in, the door's open,' a faint voice called out and he frowned, turned the rusty doorknob and stepped into a dark, dingy, narrow hallway.

'We're in the front room.' Maya's voice, louder this time, came from somewhere on his right and he strode down the passageway, trying to ignore the horrible musty odour and putrid yellow wallpaper.

They couldn't live here. No way. He hadn't even seen the rest of the house and he already knew he'd have to think of some way to get Maya and Chas out of this hell hole.

'Hey,' he said, stopping in the doorway to the 'front room', a tiny box of a space which had a threadbare sofa, a small table and a smaller TV on it. Maya had taken up residence on the sofa, her ankle propped up on a cushion while Chas lay on a bunny rug on the floor next to her, fast asleep.

For some strange inexplicable reason, the cosy scene brought a lump to his throat. Him, the guy who thrived on the highs of stockbroking, the guy who handled millions on a daily basis, the guy who loved travelling, the guy who didn't have time for a wife or the responsibility a relationship entailed because he was married to his job—just the way he liked it.

Maybe the stress of Joe's death was getting to him.

'Hey, yourself. Why don't you come in and make yourself comfortable? Pull up a piece of floor and take a seat.' She smiled, a tentative movement of her lips as if she expected him to launch straight into her for living in such a hovel. 'It's not the Taj Mahal but for the price it'll do for now.'

'Uh-huh,' was all he said, using every ounce of self control not to sweep Chas into his arms, grab Maya and rush them out the door. 'How's the ankle?'

She grimaced and pointed to the walking stick propped next to her. 'Not good. I need that thing to get around and even then I'm hobbling. It hurts like the devil and the doc said I have to keep off it for a few weeks.'

'Ouch.'

Let me help you.

What about Chas?

How can you care for a toddler let alone yourself?

How can you live here?

The questions flashed through his mind so quickly he had to clench his jaw to stop himself from blurting them out. After a few seconds when he'd calmed enough, he said, 'How are you managing with Chas?'

'Barely,' she said, glancing down at her sleeping son with that special serene expression she got whenever the boy's name was mentioned: the expression that made him feel as if he was missing out on something; the expression that allayed his fears about her maternal instincts. 'He stayed up at the Gould house while I was checked out and the nanny brought him home for me.'

A light bulb went off in his head as he looked at her ankle. 'Right ankle. No driving, huh?'

'You said it.' She paused, a faint flush staining her cheeks and he stared, mesmerised.

Maya wasn't a woman who blushed. She coped with everything life dished out to her and more yet here she was, looking embarrassed about something. Interesting…

'Riley, I know I acted like an ass when you offered to help me before and I'd like to say sorry for that.'

Ah…so that was it. He bit back a grin, knowing apologies wouldn't come easily to a proud woman like her.

'Don't worry about it,' he said, hoping she'd go further and actually ask for his help. By the size of that ankle swathed in ice and bandages, she didn't have much choice.

Her blush deepened, adding lustre to her eyes and he silently cursed. Joe was barely cold in his grave and he was noticing way too many details about Maya.

'If the offer still stands, I guess I could use your help now,' she said, tilting her chin, looking him in the eye, as if daring him to pity her.

Unfortunately, pity was the furthest emotion he felt as he stared into her heart-shaped face, the too-pale skin devoid of make-up in stark contrast to the intense green of her eyes and natural rosy pink of her lips.

Those lips… Damn it, more of those details he needed to stop noticing.

'Of course the offer still stands. I can have you out of here by tonight. You can stay in a hotel till I arrange alternative housing. I can hire a full time nanny to look after Chas till you're better. I can—'

'I don't want your money!'

Anger scorched across her face and she calmed with obvious effort. He could see it in the unclenching fists, the softening of her shoulders and he bided his time, watching uncertainty war with pride, fury battle vulnerability.

She didn't speak for several moments, her gaze darting between Chas and him before she straightened her shoulders and shuffled back in the sofa, as if needing some kind of support to brace against.

'What do you want then?' he finally prompted, increasingly uncomfortable with standing in this tiny room, feeling like a giant at an elf's tea party—not knowing what to say or do, clumsy in his efforts to help.

For a moment he wondered if she'd heard him as her attention remained fixed on Chas, the intensity of maternal love etched on her face taking his breath away.

'I do want something from you.'

Maya spoke so softly he blinked several times, wondering if he'd imagined it.

'You know you only have to ask and I'll help in any way I can,' he said, sounding like a CD track stuck on repeat. He'd lost count of the number of times he'd said these words or something similar to her since Joe's death.

'Good. In that case, I want a commitment from you.'

His world tilted as the impact of her demand hit him full-on and he struggled for a response, not surprised when he came up with nothing.

CHAPTER FIVE

'I KNOW IT'S a lot to ask,' Maya rushed on, taking Riley's stunned expression as an instant 'no' and intent on making him see this from her point of view, 'but I need a time commitment from you. I can't take your money; it just wouldn't be right. That woman at the funeral—'

'Forget about that. You shouldn't listen to spiteful gossip or let it affect your decisions.'

Maya shook her head, wondering how long he'd stick around when he heard the rest of her proposal. 'That woman was only reiterating what a lot of people in this city think. If you help me out by putting us up in a hotel, paying our bills, paying for accommodation, don't you think it only adds fuel to the fire? Can't you see that I won't let the slightest bit of scandal taint Chas?'

She looked down at her sleeping son, a tiny smile quivering around his mouth as he dreamed and she fervently wished that her son's dreams were filled with happiness and light, the antithesis of her own most nights.

'I don't want my son exposed to any more talk than

necessary and I already know what he'll have to face when he's older.'

Confusion clouded Riley's eyes, turning them stormy pewter rather than their usual startling blue of a Melbourne sky on a sunny day. 'What will he have to face?'

'People *talk*. They're talking now. About Joe's drink-driving, about how he was lucky to only kill himself and not some other innocent person, about his gambling, about me...' She trailed off, afraid she'd said too much.

She didn't want to get into the whole 'woe-is-me' thing with Riley. If he'd thought that woman at the funeral had been harsh, it was nothing to what she'd heard doing the rounds about her previously.

'What are people saying about you?'

His voice had taken on a hard edge and she should've known he wouldn't let this go. Riley was a go-getter, the type of guy who made things happen, who left no stone unturned. Just her luck...

She shifted under the scrutiny of his stare, silently cursing her sprained ankle and her inability to escape.

'I'm a horse strapper, Joe was part of the owner's circle. I kept working after we met, he pursued me relentlessly till I moved into his condo. I got knocked up, Joe proposed. You do the math. What do you think people are saying?'

She couldn't keep the bitterness from her voice as the truth echoed in her head. Yes, people had said all that but there was only one reason Joe had pursued her and he'd made it all too plain on the night he'd written himself off. He'd given her a glaring reminder of her failure as a woman to attract a man, a clear message as to why a guy in Joe's social circle would ever look twice at a scruffy tomboy like her. His words, not hers.

'The people who matter don't think like that. And when Chas is old enough, the gossip around Joe's death will've blown over.' Riley straightened, as if ready to don a superhero cape and protect his nephew against any hint of scandal to come his way.

'You don't know what it's like,' she said, her voice barely above a whisper, wishing she didn't have to tell him any of this but needing him to understand. 'I bet you've never faced the cruel taunts from kids because your shoes had holes in them or your clothes were two sizes too small.' Or been beaten black and blue in fights defending a mother who'd turned up at the school gate in hair rollers and a nightie because she'd been too drunk to remember to get dressed. 'Kids can be nasty and I don't want Chas to face the tiniest hint of gossip. It's soul-destroying for a child to face innuendo and whispers and I won't have my son subjected to that.'

'But I'm family to Chas. Accepting my financial help isn't a bad thing.'

It was easy for Mr Success to stand there and say people who mattered didn't think the worst but could he say the same about himself?

'Until Joe's death, you didn't know me from Adam. Tell me you never suspected I was a gold-digger out to fleece your brother.'

His sharp intake of breath told her everything she needed to know. 'I didn't know you.'

'And what makes you think you do now?'

His gaze rested on Chas before he raised his eyes slowly to lock on to hers. 'I'm an astute businessman. I read people for a living. Let's just say you're an open book.'

'What a load of—'

'You had it tough growing up?'

She sighed, knowing she'd opened a can of worms by giving him a hint into her past and wishing she hadn't gone there.

'You could say that. We were dirt poor, lived in a variety of places similar to this one.' She tried not to cringe at the memories. Every rented hovel her mum had shuffled them into had smelt the same: old, decaying, putrid. The type of smell she'd never forgotten.

'Your parents didn't work?'

'No. I had no father and Mum was sick for so long.'

'I'm sorry,' he said, sorrow darkening his eyes.

From what she'd said, he obviously thought her mum was dead and Maya didn't bother correcting him.

In a sad way, she almost had been all those wasted years.

'Don't be. Now, if you're through with the twenty questions, can we get back to why you're here?'

'Sure. This help you wanted?'

Thankfully, he didn't push her for more. She just wished he'd lose the look of frank admiration on his face, as if she'd survived the Holocaust rather than growing up poor.

'You know I'm a horse strapper, right?'

'Right.'

'One of my charges, Material Girl, is a fancy for the

Melbourne Cup. The thing is, I'm sort of like her stable pony.'

His lips twitched, tilting up at the outer corners. 'Which means she won't eat or sleep or gallop unless you're around?'

'Exactly. I need her to win the Cup for a variety of reasons, most importantly, financial, therefore I have to be there in the next few weeks leading up to the big race. That's where you come in.'

Riley's grin lit up the dingy room as he snapped his fingers. 'Consider it done. I'll hire someone to take over your duties and you can sit around the stable issuing orders. I think you'd be great at that. Anything else?'

Maya's heart sank. He just didn't get it. She'd rather ride Albert piggyback around the stable for the next month than accept Riley's money.

'No,' she said, trying to keep a hold on her fragile temper.

'Pardon?'

'What part of no don't you understand?'

Oops, her voice rose and she calmed it with effort. What would it take to get through to this guy?

'It's the only solution that makes sense,' he said, a tiny frown creasing his brow as his smile vanished and he stared at her with growing trepidation.

She sighed and glanced at her sleeping son for inspiration. How could she convince him that she needed more than a financial solution…?

Suddenly a light bulb lit up in her head and if she could've danced a jig she would've.

'The other night you said you want to be a part of Chas's life. Is that true?'

'Of course.' His frown deepened.

'Good. Because I can't take your money and that's that. Like I said when you walked in here, I need something just as important from you and that's your time. Three weeks, to be precise, till I'm back on my feet and able to get back to work.'

He paused for a second before nodding reluctantly. 'It'll be tough but I can rearrange my schedule, get someone to mind him while I'm in meetings, set up a play area in my office. It won't be ideal but I'll get to spend some time with the little guy.' He smiled at Chas, who rolled over in his sleep into his customary bum-in-the-air position and stuck a thumb into his mouth.

Maya cleared her throat and bit the inside of her cheek to prevent herself from laughing out loud. 'Actually, you won't be *exactly* looking after Chas.'

Riley's gaze slid upwards from Chas and settled on her, the tiny characteristic frown reappearing between his eyebrows, doing nothing to detract from his good looks. 'Then what will I be doing?'

Maya grinned sheepishly and shrugged her shoulders, hoping her spur of the moment brilliant idea to challenge his ego would have the desired result.

'How good are you with horses?'

Little wonder the guy was a success in the business world. A second after the question left her lips, he started shaking his head.

'Forget it.'

She screwed up her nose, doing her best to look disgusted. 'That'd be right. You're happy to throw your money around to hire stable staff and nannies but you're afraid to get your hands dirty.'

'Don't be ridiculous.'

Her gaze locked on his with unswerving accuracy. 'Then what is it? You want to be a part of Chas's life but only from a distance? Chas will be at the Gould house and down at the stable so if you want to hang out with him, here's your chance. If you want to get to know him you need to do it on a physical and emotional level, not from some corporate skyscraper. Why don't you come down from your glass tower and see how the real people live? What have you got to lose?'

Tiny blue flecks sparked in his eyes as he opened his mouth and clamped it shut again, the smile well and truly gone from his handsome face.

'We start tomorrow morning at five. If you're not all talk and have the guts, that is,' she said, throwing down the final challenge, crossing her fingers behind her back that he'd go for it.

Riley couldn't believe it.

Sure, he'd wanted to trade his stuffy suit and tie for T-shirt and jeans every day of his stockbroking life but glancing down at his mud-splattered denim, the filthy grey T-shirt that had started out pale blue and dirt-encrusted boots, he knew this wasn't quite what he'd had in mind.

'You're doing great,' Maya said from her make-shift day bed tucked into a nearby corner of the stables, a wide grin on her face. 'Now that you've mucked out the stall, you'll be ready to give her a thorough groom when she comes back from the water walker.'

Riley stuck the broom he'd been using behind a bale of hay with particular viciousness and wiped his hands on the back of his jeans.

'Let me get this straight. You've sat around all day barking orders at me while crooning to that damn stubborn horse that has been galloped, fussed over and had a swim. Throw in the fact that I've mucked out this stall twice, swept the yard, cleaned tack, groomed, fed and all but massaged that horse, and you want me to groom her again?'

Maya's grin widened, a genuine warm gesture that slammed into his gut like a horse's hoof if he was stupid enough to stand too close. 'It's all in your job description.'

He stalked towards her, wishing he didn't have an impulse to throw her over his knee and paddle her butt. She'd been driving him nuts all week, issuing orders like a despot one minute, praising him like a toilet-trained toddler the next. Condescending and patronising sprang to mind but then it wasn't all her fault. He'd been stupid enough to take her up on her dare and look where his pride had landed him—knee-deep in hay and shovelling manure.

The woman was a menace. And this was only his first week on the job.

'Whose job description?' He squatted next to her, needing to be on eye level to have this conversation. The conversation when he said 'I quit.'

He'd pay someone to do this. It had nothing to do with getting his hands dirty and everything to do with the woman gazing at him with guileless green eyes. And dammit if she wasn't doing that whole wide-eyed-innocent-look she had down pat, the same one she'd used to coerce him into taking this on in the first place.

He couldn't spend another day with her watching him, burning a hole into his back, that look taunting him like a temptress when he knew nothing could be further from the truth.

Every illicit thought he had towards her was all in his own mind and the longer he spent in her company, the harder it was to ignore the ugly truth.

He liked Maya. Liked her a lot and spending time with her, workplace or not, was fuelling ridiculous fantasies in his head.

'You knew what the job entailed when you signed up,' she said, reaching out to pluck a hay stalk from his T-shirt, her fingers brushing his arm in the process and setting his skin alight.

He had it bad.

When an innocuous movement from a woman who saw him as friend material only, and only just, sent the blood rushing from his head down south, he knew he had to distance himself. Fast.

'Look, I know I agreed to help you out but surely there's any number of people who can do this?'

He made a vague gesture around the stable, effectively wiping the smile from her face in the process.

'No, there isn't,' she said, speaking so softly he had

to lean forward to hear her and regretting it when her subtle rose fragrance wafted over him. It was a highly evocative smell, one that overpowered the earthy tones permeating the stable.

'You're doing great and you're getting to spend time with Chas.' She sent him a bewitching smile that lit up her face. 'Besides, I can't afford to lose this job and who else would put up with me lounging around watching them work all for the sake of placating a horse?'

Steeling his heart against the vulnerability in the fathomless green pools staring at him, he said, 'I've really enjoyed seeing more of Chas and it's given me an insight into what you do. And, at the risk of one of your snappy comebacks, I'm going to pay you a compliment and say I admire you. Your grit, your determination, the way you've moved forward. But I think this cowboy's had enough of getting his hands dirty. How about I hire someone now to do the rest?'

Her smile widened as she sat back, folded her arms and looked him up and down as if he was a horse she was contemplating buying.

'That would be right. Get a bit of dirt under your fingernails, a bit of sweat on your brow and you bolt like a scared colt.' She studied her own fingernails at arm's length before returning her challenging gaze to his. 'I didn't think you had what it took, guess you proved me right. And I'll be sure to give Chas those extra cuddles he'll miss from you.'

Riley frowned. 'You don't play fair.'

'Who says I'm playing? I'm just calling it how I see

it.' She quirked an eyebrow, her sassy smile driving him to distraction. Or despair!

'Look, this just isn't me. I've got a pile of work waiting for me at the office and—'

'It's only for a few weeks. I know you think it's crazy but Material Girl won't behave if I'm not around. She goes all loopy and not just from her high energy feed. We've tried so many things but it looks like I'm her version of a stable pony. Without me, she won't run and if she doesn't run, no chance of winning the Cup and there goes my chance at securing a future for Chas. You know, that little guy who's your nephew, who you give horsey rides to around here during your breaks, who waves to you with a big grin every morning? Why would you want to lose more quality time with him?'

Her smile had vanished and her words came out in a rush as she sighed heavily at the end, imploring him to listen with a death-grip on his arm and desperation in her eyes.

What choice did he have?

Joe had often taunted him with the label 'do-gooder' ever since he'd rescued his first baby bird with a broken wing at the age of seven. Yes, he gave generously to charities and sponsored a young child in Africa but that was his way of giving something back for the abundance of wealth he'd been lucky enough to grow up with and to make since. Of course Joe hadn't seen it that way. He'd teased him about having a weak spot for the underdog, about easing his own guilty conscience at having the best.

Joe had never understood him. Ironic, considering the lengths he'd gone to in trying to compete.

'You drive a hard bargain,' he said, guessing she'd played her trump card about Chas at the end, knowing he wouldn't walk away from his nephew and their burgeoning relationship.

'Please, Riley.'

Two simple words—soft, vulnerable, shattering the last of his resistance.

He couldn't say no.

No matter how tough the next few weeks would be spending hour after hour in her presence, he'd do it, if only for Chas's sake.

'Okay, fine. Though if I'm about to step in a pile of horse doo-doo, at least let me know next time.'

Her answering smile lit up her face, adorable creases fanning out from the corners of her eyes and begging him to trace their tiny contours.

'You're on,' she said, her smile stiffening as she glanced down at her hand resting on his arm and jerked it away as if burned.

Ironic, considering he was burning up from the inside out courtesy of her hand hanging on to him as if she never wanted to let go. He understood she'd only touched him out of desperation but that didn't help his overactive imagination.

Nothing would, and the next few weeks were going to be hell, one hundred per cent pure torture.

CHAPTER SIX

'THAT GUY KNOWS his way around horses,' Albert said, jerking his head towards the stall where Riley was currently grooming Material Girl, a begrudging respect on his weather-worn face.

'Lucky for me he grew up around them.'

Maya watched Riley's rhythmic motion with the curry comb—slow, circular movements designed to remove dried sweat and stimulate blood circulation.

Unfortunately, the only stimulation that sprang to mind as she watched his hypnotic hands had her blushing and wishing Riley wasn't so darn nice.

Though nice was a pretty inadequate word to sum up what Riley was: sexy, attractive, impressive all sprang to mind, swiftly followed by two words guaranteed to put a dampener on her silly thoughts. Joe's brother.

'So tell me again what he gets out of it?'

Albert leaned against the stable door reminding her of an overprotective terrier, all five foot nothing of wiry muscles, his big-man swagger not matching his pint-size frame. His astute gaze registered Maya's blush before his focus returned to Riley. He frowned, looking as if he was ready to bare his teeth and growl.

'Riley wanted to spend some time with Chas and to help out. Pretty decent, huh?'

'Uh-huh,' said her terrier, not sounding convinced. 'So does that mean he gets a share of the hundred grand the boss promised you when the Girl wins the Cup next week?'

'She's no certainty to win. It's a tough field,' Maya said, hating the pressure on her prized charge and hating Albert's probing more. 'And if we're talking money, how about you tell me how much you jockeys squander of the millions you earn a year first?'

Albert's wry smile lit up his cheeky face. 'Touché. Yeah, it's a tough field but you want my opinion? The Girl's handling like a dream. She's cruising when she's galloping and the three thousand, two hundred metres is going to be a walk in the park for a stayer like her.'

'I hope you're right,' Maya said, her eyes drawn to Riley again as he brushed the mare from head to tail in a flicking motion. She was impressed by the care he'd taken.

Not that she'd expected anything less. From the minute he'd stepped up after Joe's death, he'd struck her as responsible, the type of guy who'd give his all to whatever task he set out to do.

'Wanna tip straight from the horse's mouth?' Albert tapped the side of his nose and winked. 'You're on a winner there.'

Maya hoped Albert meant the mare and not Riley as

he gave her a thumbs-up sign of encouragement and strutted across the yard towards the track.

Shaking her head, whether at Albert's antics or to dispel the tiny seed of awareness he'd sown in her consciousness, she limped across the stable and leaned on the stall door.

'Albert's impressed with the job you're doing.'

Riley stopped brushing the mare, patted her flank and smiled, a hundred-watt mega-smile that twisted Maya's insides into knots. And horses thought they had it bad with colic!

'Great. Nice to see my efforts to impress *Albert* have paid off.'

Darn, how did he do that—load words with meaning that weren't there? Or was that her own idiotic mind hoping he was implying that he wanted to impress her?

'Get back to work. You're not finished yet.'

'Yes, Ma'am,' he said, his swift mocking salute the perfect foil to her laughing orders.

She would miss this: the teasing, the camaraderie, the easiness of it all. Spending time with Riley, albeit in a professional arena, had been comfortable. They'd developed a closeness which she'd never had with Joe and, as hard as she tried, she couldn't stop the comparisons.

It may be wrong, it may be futile, but a small part of her had developed a teensy-weensy crush on the capable Riley over the last few weeks, a crush she had no intention of acting upon. Chas was too important for that. His future was all that mattered and there was no way a child of hers would suffer humiliation at the hands of its mother.

'How's the ankle?' he tossed over his shoulder as he squatted, lifted Material Girl's right fore foot and used a hoof pick to clean it.

'Fine. Just a bit of residual stiffness, nothing major. The doc said I'll be back to full time duties in a few days.'

And not a moment too soon, the way she'd taken to indulging in fanciful daydreams while watching Riley work.

She'd worked around men and horses her entire life but had never found any of the guys remotely attractive, yet somehow, every time Riley got within two feet of her, the smell of fresh hay combined with male sweat drove her crazy.

Add to that the fact he had a great body clearly on display in faded denim and soft cotton T-shirts, and the constant smiles he sent her way, and her imagination was on overload and in definite danger of short-circuiting.

'Is that the people's doc or the horse doc?'

'The only doc I trust,' she said, flexing her ankle several times, amazed at the progress she'd made thanks to 'the horse doc' as Riley labelled the stable's resident vet, Doc Larkspur. 'I've soaked my ankle in that goop he gave me every night and it's done the trick. Even you can't deny that, Mr Conservative.'

He straightened and moved around Material Girl but not before she'd seen the smile that hovered around his mouth vanish in a second.

'Guess you're right. Though I swear that blackish-greeny muck looked like something I've been scooping up in the stable rather than a remedy for inflamed tendons.'

He'd squatted down on the mare's far side and Maya

couldn't see him. She heard his flat, controlled tone and wondered what it was about.

She'd been teasing with the Mr Conservative remark. Heck, he openly confessed to being a serious business-oriented type—one of the qualities she admired about him. Then again, he didn't know that and she had no intention of letting him in on the secret.

'Whatever, it worked. I thought you'd be rapt. You can leave all this mucking about, no pun intended, and head back to the skyscrapers you love so much.'

To her surprise, he stood up and glared at her over the mare. 'For a person who hates other people judging her, you're doing a fine job of assuming to know a lot about me.'

His jibe hurt—a lot more than it should—and she racked her brain for some throwaway comment to fling at him to show she didn't care. Instead, she opened her mouth and the first words that popped into her head came out.

'I thought I'd learned a lot about you.'

'You thought wrong,' he snapped, pocketing the pick and wiping his hands on a dusty rag he pulled from the waistband of his jeans.

'Oo-kay.'

Maya didn't know where to look. Staring at Riley's closed-off face wasn't an option so she chose the next best thing, the mare's hind quarters. Fitting actually, as Riley was acting like a horse's ass.

'Think what you like, but at the end of the day I'm not the guy you claim to know so much about,' he said, closing the stall door with a resounding thud as he stormed past her and out of the stable.

Riley stomped around the yard, sweeping as if his life depended on it and wishing he could get in his car and drive away. He'd never been a hoon but a decent screechy exit, leaving flying gravel in his wake sounded damn good at the moment, totally in sync with his foul mood.

However, he had responsibilities, namely taking Maya and Chas home and since when did Mr Responsible shirk his duties?

He was a fool. An A-1 first class fool.

He'd thought he could steel himself against Maya these last few weeks. If he concentrated hard enough on the job and ignored her constant presence, he could get through their enforced proximity with flying colours.

For a smart guy, he'd turned into a dumb schmuck.

Concentrating on his work hadn't been the problem; dealing with his attraction for Maya had. Though there was nothing remotely romantic about scooping horse droppings and mucking out stalls, he'd grown to enjoy the time he'd spent with her in the cool, dim stable, surrounded by softly neighing horses and the scent of hay.

The stupid part was that he'd enjoyed it so damn much he'd started creating ridiculous fantasies in his head, working out how he could prolong his involvement in her life now that his knight-in-shiningarmour gig was coming to an end.

'You ready to leave?'

He stopped slamming the broom into the dust and

looked up, momentarily stunned by the enticing vision of Maya, dressed in old denim and a faded red and white plaid shirt, propped against a post with a chuckling Chas in her arms.

He wanted her.

Right here, right now.

And the knowledge smashed into his consciousness, leaving him rooted to the spot and unable to broach the short distance separating them.

'Car,' Chas chortled, waving a chubby fist in his direction and smiling. Riley's heart contracted, knowing how much he'd grown to love his nephew.

'You heard the little man. It's time for us to go home.'

Maya spoke softly, as if testing his mood and he couldn't blame her after the way he'd stormed out.

However, worse than his feeling like an idiot was the fact she'd included him in the 'us' to go home.

'Sure thing,' he said, not quite meeting her eyes as he stored the broom, had a brief word with the stable manager and did a final check on Material Girl, which basically involved a fond pat on her nose. Ironically, Maya wasn't the only female he'd miss when he went back to stockbroking. He'd always loved horses but there was something special about 'The Girl' as everyone called one of the top fancies for the Melbourne Cup.

'I'll meet you at the car, okay?'

He nodded at Maya, unable to tear his eyes away as she hobbled towards his car, holding Chas's hand as he tottered beside her on the uneven terrain.

Shaking his head, he shrugged into his jacket and followed them.

He'd overreacted, taking his frustration out on Maya. Not one of his brightest moves.

Then again, spending all this time around her, whether helping out or not, had been none too smart either.

Time to wise up. Starting now.

Maya hated the awkward silence between her and Riley. Usually their car trips home at the end of the day were filled with chatter and laughter, punctuated with gurgles and the odd 'ma-ma' from Chas in the back seat. But not today. Something had soured Riley's easygoing mood and she had an uncomfortable feeling she knew exactly what that was.

Her big mouth. She'd scared him, implying she knew him, and he'd reacted accordingly, putting as much emotional distance between them as possible. A predictable pattern, one she easily recognised. It had happened to her repeatedly throughout her life: the closer she'd tried to get to her mum, the harder her mum pushed her away. Joe had been the same.

She should've learned from her life experiences yet here she was, reaching out to another human being again just because he'd shown her a little kindness. She'd be better off sticking with horses. They understood her a lot better than anyone else on the planet and she didn't destroy her relationships with them.

'Here we are,' Riley said, sliding to a stop outside her place, not switching off the engine as he usually did.

'Thanks.'

Maya toyed with her seatbelt, furiously marshalling her thoughts. She couldn't leave things between them like this. Tomorrow was Saturday and she'd be back at work on Monday, without Riley. He'd done so much for her and what had she done in return? Scared the living daylights out of the man by implying she knew him better than he knew himself.

'Would you like to come in for dinner?' she blurted, issuing the invitation in a rush before she chickened out. 'It's the least I can do after the way you've helped us out the last few weeks.'

Riley's long fingers drummed the steering wheel as if he couldn't wait to get away. 'Thanks, but I've got other plans tonight.'

'Oh. Right. Of course you have,' she said, fumbling with the door latch in her hurry to escape the car. 'I'll let you go.'

Riley nodded, sending her a cursory glance before turning to Chas in the back seat. 'You be good for your mama, okay?'

Chas grinned and shoved his fist in his mouth, the picture of bashful innocence, and she smiled, knowing one guy in this world wouldn't let her down.

'Come on, little man. Let's get you inside.' She unbuckled the child restraints and swung Chas into her arms, inhaling his unique smell of powder and no-tears shampoo, knowing the two of them would be okay.

Thanks to Riley.

He'd given them a fighting chance by helping her out

these last few weeks and she owed him. Not that he wanted a bar of her gratitude.

Lifting Chas on to her left hip, she closed the door and waved, wondering why the front façade of her rundown house suddenly seemed more derelict than ever. She rarely noticed the peeling paint or rusty screen door but, then again, Riley usually kept up a steady stream of conversation, adding entertaining to the list of his endearing qualities as he helped her and Chas into the house. While she'd been stuck using the walking stick he'd bathed Chas, fed them both and generally gone above and beyond the call of duty.

Yes, he was Chas's uncle and she knew that had been the main motivation for his chivalrous behaviour but it had been nice to dream that he cared about her too. For a woman who'd been starved of affection most of her life, she'd lapped it up.

Riley tooted the horn and Chas squealed with delight, wriggling frantically in her arms as he waved at his uncle.

Wishing she didn't feel so dejected, she took a step towards the house as the passenger window slid down in a smooth electronic glide and a blast of cool air-conditioning hit her.

'Are you and Chas free on Sunday?' Riley leaned across the passenger seat, craning his neck to look up at her.

'Uh-huh,' she said, ignoring the instant firing of her pulse at his question.

She shouldn't have been surprised. The Riley she knew wouldn't turn his back on Chas no matter how much he wanted to distance himself from her.

'Good. I'll come by and we can go for a picnic.'

'Sounds great,' she said, hugging Chas tighter as he tried to climb through the open window, reaching out for his uncle with increasingly loud yells. Maya was almost using him as a human shield against the surge of emotion that had her heart flip-flopping in a way it hadn't done since Joe.

'Later, little man,' Riley said, blowing Chas a kiss before lifting his too-blue gaze to focus on her, an unfathomable expression in their depths.

'See you Sunday.'

He didn't smile, he didn't say much but there was something in the way he looked at her that had her dreaming the impossible dream.

'Okay.'

She straightened, cuddling a distraught Chas and watching Riley drive away, her emotions in turmoil.

CHAPTER SEVEN

WHEN MAYA OPENED the door to Riley's knock at eleven a.m. on Sunday morning she could barely summon the energy to notice how incredible he looked in navy shorts, a white polo shirt and brown boat shoes. Nor did she pay particular attention to the monstrous picnic basket at his feet. Instead, she managed a weary smile and gestured him in.

'Everything okay?'

'Rough night.'

He didn't push her for details, picking up the basket and following her in. She took him through to the tiny kitchen, grimacing at what he must see: empty pizza box on the bench, unwashed dishes piled in the sink, stack of newspapers covering the table and the remnants of Chas's cereal breakfast splattered over every surface within throwing distance of his high chair.

'Take a seat if you can find one,' she said, padding across the kitchen to flick the switch on the kettle. 'Want a cuppa?'

'How about you sit and I'll make it?'

Her glance flew to his, looking for judgement or condemnation, only to find concern. She could've argued
the point that she wasn't entirely helpless but right now,
she couldn't summon the energy.

'Be my guest,' she said, plopping into a wobbly
wooden chair and rolling her neck in semi-circles to
ease the tension.

'Where's Chas?'

'At the Goulds'. I was called into work early this
morning, some sort of scare with the Girl, so I took
him along.'

'And left him there?'

She heard the censure in his voice but didn't care.
Now that she'd sat down, she couldn't get up if her life
depended on it and she really needed that cup of tea, the
one he was making for her. Insulting the chief tea-maker
at this point in time would not be a smart move.

'Brett saw I was dead on my feet and offered for the
nanny to mind Chas for a few hours. His boys are being
looked after today too because of the lead up to the Cup
so I took him up on the offer.'

Riley placed a steaming mug of English Breakfast tea
with a dash of milk and two sugars, just the way she
liked it, in front of her and she made a frantic grab at it,
practically inhaling the sweet caffeine hit in her desperation for a soothing sip.

'What happened?'

She savoured the intense flavour and the instant pick-
me-up it gave her, cradling the mug in her hands and
tucking her bare feet on to the rung beneath her.

'Chas was teething last night. Slight fever, runny nose, screaming in agony, the works. We both got about two hours sleep max and then Brett called, asking if I could make it in for the Girl's gallop.'

Riley sent her a startled look. 'You were at the track at five this morning?'

'No choice,' she mumbled, taking another healthy gulp of tea and closing her eyes as the warmth infused her cold bones.

'You could've called me.'

Her eyes flew open and she wondered if half the annoyance she felt at his throwaway comment showed in her eyes. Joe had always said her face was an open book. Pity he'd had no interest in reading the fine print.

'You think? After the way you acted on Friday, do you reckon I would've been comfortable calling you in the middle of the night?'

A tiny frown creased his brow as his eyes darkened to a stormy midnight. 'You can call me any time regardless of when or where. You know that.'

'No, I don't.'

How could she, when he'd withdrawn from her, establishing a wall she was too nervous to breach?

He ran a hand through his hair, sending dark spikes skyward, and shook his head.

'I'm not Joe,' he said softly, pushing away from the table and heading to the sink to stare out the small grimy window overlooking the minuscule back yard, which was strangled by weeds.

'Obviously.'

Joe wouldn't be making her cups of tea, let alone offering to help her. Though he'd openly encouraged her work, he hadn't lifted a finger to make it easier on her even after Chas was born, hence the nanny arrangement at the Goulds'.

She'd been so stupid.

If she'd realised the reason behind Joe's fervent support of her job right from the start, none of this would've happened.

Though Riley was right about one thing: he wasn't Joe. He was ten times the man Joe had ever been and, rather than push him away, she needed him onside if only for Chas's sake. She'd grown up without any extended family and she wouldn't deprive Chas of the chance to know his uncle because of some hang-up she had.

Riley turned back to face her, uncertainty lending his face a vulnerability she'd never seen before. 'Look, I'm sorry about Friday. It wasn't your fault. Guess I didn't know how to handle the possibility of not being needed any more and I took it out on you.'

Maya rubbed a hand across her eyes. Yes, she was sleep-deprived but she was sure Riley had just admitted that he *wanted* her to need him.

'Can you say that again?' she asked, finishing the rest of her tea in record time. She really needed to stay awake long enough to hear this.

'I've been like this my whole life. Playing the dependable big brother to Joe, taking on as much responsibility as possible, helping anyone and everyone. I thrive on it. Joe said I was a control freak but it's not

like that. I like helping out. I like being here for...
Chas.'

His pause caused hope to unfurl around her heart that
he'd actually meant to say, I like being here for you.

'But you know the crazy thing? I was there for Joe
all his life but, when he needed me the most, I took the
easy option. I brushed him off.'

Riley resumed pacing, which constituted a few steps
left and right in the claustrophic confines of the kitchen.

Suddenly, a flash of clarity made Riley's involvement
with them clear. 'So that's why you're helping us out?
You feel guilty for not being there for Joe?'

It made perfect sense and she'd been a fool to contemplate any other motivation for Riley's being there for
her than his connection to Chas and his love for Joe.

He stopped and dropped into the chair right next to
her, way too close for comfort, making her all too aware
of her grimy jeans and thin cotton top.

'Initially that was a driving force. Though now, my
being around has nothing to do with Joe or any guilt-
trip I'm on.'

His intent gaze, combined with his proximity, set off
alarm bells in her brain.

He was too close.

And she had nowhere to run, let alone the energy to
do so.

'Then why are you here?'

'Because I care about Chas. He's family and you're
a part of that,' he said, his steady gaze sending her pulse

racing and her stomach dropping in a sickening free-fall without the safety net of her usual reticence.

For in that moment, she wondered whether Riley's caring was about more than familial responsibility, whether he sensed the strange undercurrent of emotion that had developed between them over the last few weeks.

'Chas is lucky to have an uncle like you,' she said, choosing her words carefully, not prepared to delve into anything deeper when her mind was fuzzy and craving sleep.

Rubbing a hand over gritty eyes while stifling a yawn with the other, she sank further into her chair, wishing he'd take off so she could have a much needed nap.

'Guess you're not up for a picnic?'

'You guessed right.'

This time, she couldn't prevent a wide yawn from escaping and almost grimaced at the picture she must present: dishevelled appearance, hair in scruffy pigtails, dark circles of fatigue under her eyes and a yawn that would do the big clown at Luna Park proud.

He smiled, a gentle smile full of understanding, and it took all her willpower not to snuggle against his broad chest and ask him to take her to her room and tuck her in for a nap like she'd seen him do with Chas.

'In that case, how about I collect Chas from the Goulds', take him away for some fresh air and give you a few more free hours to catch up on some beauty sleep?'

'That would be great.'

She mustered a tired smile and pushed away from the table, standing with the effort of a ninety-year-old with arthritis. 'He'll have a nap around three, so if you bring him back by then he won't get too grumpy on you.'

'I can handle the little guy.'

She must've swayed on her feet for his arms shot out and grabbed hold of her waist, steadying her.

However, there was nothing remotely steady about her heartbeat. It jumped and bucked like a stalled stallion, throwing in a few kicks for good measure as her hands reached out instinctively to brace on his forearms.

Like everything about him, his forearms were strong, solid and warm. Hot, in fact, the heat branding the skin of her palms till she almost melded to him.

If she weren't so tired she would've pulled away the instant she registered how good it felt to touch him but instead she just stood there like a dummy, their gazes locked, something akin to electricity arcing between them in the dreary kitchen.

'Bed really seems like a good idea right about now,' she said, all but pushing him away in her haste to escape the tension-fraught situation and seek solace in slumber. If he didn't haunt her dreams, that was.

'You're right,' he said, his lips curving into a teasing smile and her stomach flip-flopped with embarrassment as she realised what she'd said.

'Okay, now that we've established I'm a very tired woman who can't string two coherent words together, it's time you headed off on that picnic,' she said, grateful he hadn't taken her poorly-phrased statement for an invitation as many guys would've.

But then, Riley Bourke wasn't like many guys, at least not the ones she'd ever known.

His grin broadened and he leaned forward to drop a chaste peck on her cheek. 'I'm off. Now, you hit that bed while I spend some quality time with my nephew and we'll see you around three.'

She managed a tired nod, waiting till the front door closed behind him to ponder her irrational disappointment that his farewell kiss had been so brief and filled with a despondency that, no matter how great a guy Riley was, he had no place in her life other than as Chas's uncle.

Riley chased, tickled, cajoled and cuddled Chas all afternoon, in awe of Maya and what she did every day to care for an active toddler like his nephew. Chas was a dervish, a never-ending bundle of energy who craved attention—like all kids—and threw a tantrum when he didn't get it. He'd heard of the terrible twos but it looked as if this little man was getting in some practice early.

'Go-go,' Chas said, tears filling his eyes as he reached up his chubby arms from the plaid blanket Riley had spread under a massive oak in the Botanic Gardens.

'You've had enough too, huh?' Riley picked Chas up and cuddled him, contentment seeping through his body and tugging on his heart-strings.

He'd never had any dreams to find a wife and have kids, happy to think that if it happened, it happened. Besides, he'd been married to his career for longer than he cared to remember and bailing Joe out of one scrape after another was like caring for a kid anyway.

However, the last few weeks with Chas had been in-credible and he'd bonded with the little guy quicker than he'd anticipated. Initially, he'd attributed it to guilt at letting Joe down by burying his head in business but he'd quickly realised that wasn't true. Like his father, Chas was a charmer. After all, he'd charmed his uncle into loving him unconditionally before Riley could even blink.

'Go,' Chas murmured, his bottom lip quivering in a classic move preceding a lusty lungful.

'Okay, little man. We're going.'

Tossing the blanket on top of the picnic basket, he hauled Chas on to his hip as he'd seen Maya do a hundred times and picked up the basket with his free hand, chuckling ruefully at the domestic picture he must present. If the guys at the office could see him now…

Not that they'd seen him for weeks and, if he had his way, they wouldn't see him for a while longer. Joe's death, while futile and tragic, had given him a long-overdue wake-up call. Business had become his life, a substitute for many things, including a possible relation-ship and all it entailed.

He'd liked it that way. He understood the corporate world, which was more than he could say about women.

He'd tried to be rational about the whole Maya situ-ation to the extent that he'd deliberately pushed her away last Friday. It had been petty but when she'd labelled him as being some kind of jackass eager to dump them and get back to his previous life, he'd almost lost it.

He'd been feeling pretty down anyway at the thought

that she wouldn't need him any more and her jibe hadn't helped matters.

She'd invited him for dinner; he'd told her the barefaced lie that he had plans. Yeah, plans with his laptop and mobile to connect with the office and catch up; real scintillating stuff. But what made it worse was the hurt he'd seen in her eyes and the realisation that his boorish behaviour had put it there.

So he'd come up with the spur of the moment picnic idea. Glancing down at the drowsy child in his arms, he knew that a boy's day out wasn't quite what he'd had in mind at the time and that his idea of a perfect Sunday picnic would've included Maya.

In a way, not having her here wasn't too bad considering that insane moment in her kitchen when he'd wanted to haul her into his arms and kiss her senseless. She'd looked so fragile, so helpless, and the feel of her soft hands gripping on to him for grim death had awakened his protective instincts in a big way.

Though his motives weren't entirely altruistic. He'd tried holding her at arm's length, tried playing the concerned friend and the knight in shining armour, but when he got down to it, he wanted her: wrapped in his arms, clinging to him, needing him out of passion rather than for compassion.

Chas made a soft mewling noise as he fell into a light sleep and Riley kissed him, placed him gently in the car seat and fastened the seat belt, gazing in wonder at the little boy who had wormed his way into his heart without trying.

Business may have been his life, but, inhaling Chas's soft fragrance, seeing the tiny smile curling his cherubic lips, Riley knew that his nephew had shifted his focus for the better.

Making millions was one thing, making this precious little guy chuckle another.

Whichever way he looked at it, he was smitten.

And, deep down, he wondered if Chas was the only one who'd captured his attention away from his career and on to matters closer to home.

CHAPTER EIGHT

'YOU'RE COMING TONIGHT, right?'

Maya ignored Albert momentarily and continued sponging Material Girl's flank, using a sweat scraper to clear off any excess water.

'I don't have anything to wear,' she said deadpan, knowing that as Albert had helped her move he had seen the plastic bags containing the remnants of a designer wardrobe Joe had bought for her at the start of their relationship.

Ironic, considering everything else he'd given her had been repossessed, leaving her with a few fancy glad rags she'd rarely wear.

'As if.'

Albert snorted, doing a fine impersonation of the mare that would run in the Melbourne Cup tomorrow, the same mare whose ears pricked from side to side as if listening to their conversation. 'You'd look good in a hessian sack.'

Sluicing the last of the water from the mare, Maya gave her a gentle pat and wiped her hands before turning to the jockey who had partial control over her fate tomorrow.

'Thanks, I think. Anyway, I have to go to keep an eye on you. Don't want some bimbo spiking your drink and ruining our chances of taking home the Cup.'

'Bimbo? I'll have you know my taste in women is improving. I haven't dated a model or a soapie star for at least a month.'

Maya chuckled and slipped a fine mesh cooler over Material Girl to keep the mare warm while she dried. 'Maybe there's hope for you yet.'

'What about you? Wild horses wouldn't keep me away from seeing you and Mr Fancy Pants make a grand entrance.'

To her annoyance, heat flushed her cheeks and she tried to hide her blush by bending down and inspecting the mare's feed.

'Brett invited Riley last week and it makes sense for us to come together. We're friends.'

'Friends? Riiiight.' Albert sniggered, an aggravating sound that had her wishing the mare would give him a swift hoof right where it hurt the most.

'So that's why the guy takes a few weeks off from his own hotshot job to wake up with the birds and muck out horse poo. Because you're just *friends*.'

Maya straightened and pinned Albert with a glare that would've shrunk a giant down to his current height. 'Riley is family to Chas, a responsibility he doesn't take lightly. So yes, we're friends. We have to be for Chas's sake.'

Albert took a step towards her, laying a soothing hand on the mare, which had skittered sideways at Maya's raised voice. 'And what about your sake?'

Maya dropped her gaze, finding the hay beneath her feet infinitely more interesting than her friend's probing stare at that moment. 'Honestly? It's nice to have someone I can rely on, someone I know I can trust.'

'And?'

'And what?'

'Come off it, Eddy. We've worked together too long for you to treat me like an idiot. I've seen you with this guy and, let me tell you, he seems interested in more than just friendship.'

She raised stricken eyes to Albert, not sure whether to hope that he was wrong or wish that he was right. She'd grown attached to Riley, had valued his help with Chas, but what if he expected more....

'You're wrong.'

'What if I'm not?' Albert softened his voice. 'You could do a lot worse, you know. And, like it or not, you need to think about your future.'

'And your point is?'

'For a hotshot, this Riley chap seems like a decent sort of a guy. As you said yourself, he's family to Chas. Why don't you give him a chance?'

'Because we're friends and that's that!' she blurted, hating how cool and logical Albert sounded, annoyed with him for planting tiny seeds of hope that could grow to beanstalk proportion given encouragement.

If this was only about her, she might've considered throwing caution to the wind and seeing if there was more behind her bizarre attraction to Riley.

But she couldn't. She had Chas to think about, her

precious child who would never face a hint of scandal or shame that could taint him if she became involved with his uncle.

No matter how perfect Riley was, how considerate, how sexy, she would never put her feelings in front of her child's wellbeing.

She wasn't her mother.

'Just friends, huh?'

Clamping down the urge to stomp her feet in frustration like Chas about to have a tantrum, she said, 'That's right. Now, why don't you concentrate on not tripping over your two left feet at the Ball tonight and getting this lovely lady first past the winning post tomorrow.'

'I'll be sure to save you a dance tonight,' he said, tipping his hat in her direction before heading towards the door, his cocky grin not slipping an inch despite her brush-off. 'As for winning the race tomorrow, we can't lose. See you at the Ball with your glad rags on.'

He waved and sauntered out the door, one of Melbourne's leading jockeys at the top of his game, his big talk more than making up for his short stature. However, in this case, his talk was wrong.

She didn't have feelings for Riley.

She'd grown dependent on him, sure, but she hadn't had much option considering her torn ankle ligaments, what the possible prize money would mean to Chas's future and his interest in getting to know his nephew.

If it had been her choice, she would've spurned Riley Bourke the minute he'd offered her money and never looked back. Instead, she'd had to eat humble pie—a heavy serving which had given her a distinct case of indigestion.

Just friends, huh?

Albert's words echoed in her head, taunting her.

If having more than a friendship with Riley could potentially hurt Chas, she wouldn't go there.

Uh-uh. From now on it was her and Chas against the world and if Riley wanted to do the uncle thing, fine by her.

As for the weird attraction simmering between them, she'd ignore it.

Simple.

Maya's high heels clicked against the marble floor as she walked into the bar to meet Riley, trying to stop casting nervous sideways glances at herself in the floor to ceiling mirrors lining the entranceway.

For a girl who lived in jodhpurs and flannel shirts, she loved dressing up. The whole make-up, slinky fabric, strappy shoes transformation had always served to make her feel like a new woman and if there was ever a night she needed to feel that way, tonight was it.

The Cup Eve Ball at the Palladium was one of the social events of the Melbourne season, where horse racing people mixed with society in a glittering gala designed to dazzle. Two years ago to the day it had succeeded—though that night she'd been more dazzled by Joe than the event. Dazzled and frazzled and swept into a life-changing series of events which were still throwing her the odd curve ball.

One of which was heading towards her right now at an alarming rate of knots.

'Wow, you look incredible.'

Riley's eyes glowed with pleasure as his gaze swept from the top of her head where she'd piled her curls in a loose top-knot, to the bottom of her feet, her iridescent pink-painted toe nails poking out from silver sandals, and back up again.

'Amazing what a bit of make-up can do,' she said, trying not to shuffle from one foot to the other under his intense scrutiny.

'You're beautiful. And it has nothing to do with that evil dress or your tasteful make-up.'

Though his compliment warmed her, she didn't feel beautiful. She'd never felt beautiful.

Certainly not in the grubby hand-me-down charity shop clothes she'd been forced to wear throughout her childhood. Nor later when Joe's charming mask had dropped and he'd poked fun at her post-baby shape and penchant for jeans and T-shirts instead of designer discomfort.

Determined to ignore the past tonight, she fixed a bright smile on her face and said, 'Evil?'

Heat sizzled between them as he reached out and slowly ran his hand over the soft fabric clinging to her waist. 'This dress is the epitome of evil, from its colour to its cut. The thoughts it's going to elicit in every man who sees you in it tonight…'

His low husky voice mesmerised her. She'd never heard him speak like this let alone look at her in such a brazen way. She could usually handle the cool, serious, all-business Riley. Suave Riley had her in a mind-spinning dither!

Eager to keep the mood light and feeling exceedingly out of her depth with this new flirty version of Riley—especially since he looked mouth-wateringly sexy in a designer tux—she said, 'Strapless is in and purple's all the rage at the moment. So if being trendy is evil, that's me.'

His eyes glittered with amusement as he offered her his elbow, a quaint old-fashioned gesture that somehow suited him. 'There's nothing remotely evil about you. Unless you count that mean streak that made me pick up every last horse dropping at the stable when any number of hands could've done it. Shall we go in and have that pre-dinner drink?'

She stiffened at his mention of a drink, an old habit she hadn't been able to shake no matter how many times she watched the guys at work share a quiet beer or Brett offer his employees the finest champagne if any of his horses won a big race.

'Maya?'

Snapping back to the present, she slipped her hand into the crook of his elbow. 'Sorry. This is my first night out since Chas was born and I keep wondering how he is.'

A semi-lie. She had constantly been thinking about her darling little boy and how he was. He'd never been apart from her at night before and, though he was comfortable with the nanny at the Goulds' house—familiar surroundings to him—she couldn't wait for tonight to be over. She wanted to pick him up and rush home,

cocoon herself in her own environment, away from
prying eyes and wagging tongues and people who had
known Joe and found her lacking in every respect.

How Cinderella had braved the masses, she'd never
know.

'Don't take this the wrong way, but don't you think
you're a tad overprotective of Chas?' Riley led her to a
cosy corner table overlooking the Yarra River and the
sparkling city lights of Melbourne on the opposite bank.
'He's in safe hands in a place he feels secure. Why don't
you relax?'

She snatched her hand away from its nestling place
on his arm and plopped ungraciously into a low-slung
chair, forgetting she wasn't dressed for comfort until her
satin bodice slid across her breasts, which had her
making a frantic grab at it.

'I don't remember asking you for parenting advice,'
she said, her voice icy while she surreptitiously tugged
the bodice up, knowing this dress had been a bad idea.

'I'm not trying to give you parenting advice. You're
a great mum—anyone can see that—but I'm worried
about you. You work long hours in a tough physical job
and you spend your limited down time looking after a
boisterous toddler.'

He reached for her hand before thinking better of it
and leaning back in his chair opposite. His recoil
might've had something to do with her stiffly folded
arms and rigid posture, not to mention the semi-growl
simmering in the back of her throat like a lioness ready
to tear apart anyone who threatened her cub.

'You've just said this is your first night out in fourteen months and that's not right. I can't begin to know what Joe was thinking in not giving you some much needed time out but I can make an accurate judgement on what I see now, and what I see is a woman on the edge. A woman who is burned out, a woman doing her best to keep it all together for the sake of her child without thought to what happens if she goes under.'

Maya should've been furious. She should've ignored him, rebuffed him or laughed off his concern. Instead, the unthinkable happened and tears began to well up. How could he sum up her situation so perfectly? Joe had ignored her for over a year, not caring what happened to her or their son.

'Chas is everything to me,' she said softly, blinking rapidly to dispel the tears that threatened to seep down her cheeks and ruin her make-up job.

This time Riley didn't hesitate to take her hand, his strong grip infusing her with confidence. 'I know, but you have to start thinking about yourself. The little guy is adorable but he's exhausting too. One picnic and I had to rest up for a week.' His mock grimace was designed to make her smile and she managed a slight twitch of her glossed lips.

'Being a mother is amazing. It's what I want to do and I want to do it well. Yeah, I'm exhausted all the time but I can handle it.'

'I'm not questioning your ability to handle anything but I am worried that you're on the brink of collapsing.'

He traced an index finger under her eyes, his gentle

touch raising goose-bumps along her bare skin. 'As gorgeous as you are without make-up, I know this stuff hides the fatigue I usually see here. And here.'

His finger dropped to the corners of her mouth, tracing their outline with infinite slowness, creating warmth which spread through her body with lansguorous ease. 'Your lips are the stuff fantasies are made of so why am I used to seeing them compressed rather than smiling?'

Her mouth dried at the nearness of his fingers and the power of his words. Riley dropped his hand, his expanding pupils a clear indication that he felt as rattled as she did.

He thought her lips were fantasy material?

Oh, boy! Maybe he needed to rest up more than she did.

'You're a young woman. You should smile more, you should enjoy life, and that includes doing more than working with horses and raising Chas.'

At least he'd distracted her from crying and as she struggled between wanting to tell him where he could stick his judgement calls and hugging him for caring, a waiter came to take their order.

'A lime and soda for me, please,' she said, jumping in quickly before he could ask what she wanted, hating the surprised look or the 'cheap date' comments that followed when people realised she didn't drink alcohol.

'Bourbon on the rocks,' Riley said, not looking in the least surprised at her choice while she struggled to hide her revulsion at his.

Though at least it wasn't Scotch.

'So, at the risk of you doing more of that lip compressing thing, why don't you go away for a weekend or overnight and leave Chas with me? He'll be fine and you'll come back refreshed and relaxed. What do you say?'

Instinctively, she found her lips thinning and forced them into a smile instead. 'He'll fret.'

He leaned over and recaptured her hand in his, making her more jittery than she had been seconds ago when he'd been tracing her lips with his finger. 'Don't you mean *you'll* fret?'

'A bit of both, I guess,' Maya said, wishing his reassuring touch didn't feel so good and that he'd stop staring at her with those blue eyes that could melt any red-blooded woman at twenty paces or less. 'Thanks for the offer, but—'

'Think massages, spa baths, Vichy showers—'

'Vichy what?' She knew what a Vichy shower was but she couldn't believe a guy like Riley did.

'I'm a metrosexual,' he said, grinning broadly.

His grip hadn't loosened and she studiously avoided looking at their joined hands while simultaneously trying to ignore the startlingly vivid image of Riley having a massage under a shower of warm water jets. A very naked Riley.

'So the workaholic is giving me advice on how to unwind, huh?'

'I'm just telling it how it is. You need a break and I'm offering that to you. What do you say?'

With his blue eyes fixed on her face, his hand clasping hers as if he'd never let go and his lips curved in a warm caring smile, her resistance to the idea of leaving Chas even for one night faded.

Riley was right. She needed a break desperately and until now, she hadn't trusted anyone enough to leave her precious son with them overnight.

Yet here was the perfect opportunity to recharge her batteries, knowing that Chas would be in safe hands.

Strong, capable hands by the feel of them clasped around her own.

She sighed and found herself responding to his smile with a tentative one of her own. 'Okay. Sounds like a plan.'

'Great. How about next weekend?'

'Gee, you're pushy.'

'And you're not going to wriggle out of this,' he said, leaning closer, infusing her personal space with his presence, making her wish that the two of them could remain in this intimate bubble away from the pressures of the everyday world for ever.

'Who's wriggling?' Maya said, doing just that as she subtly slid back from him and pulled her hand out of his. She needed to establish some much-needed distance between them before she did something silly like lean into him for a cuddle.

He'd crawled under her defences tonight. She'd planned on spending an obligatory hour at the Ball at the most, including this pre-dinner drink, knowing that spending time with Riley on a night like this—two years to the day since she'd met Joe—would be tough.

Not because of Joe's memory—she'd come to terms with her faded feelings for Joe a long time before his death—but because of Riley, for the exact reasons that flashed through her mind now.

He's considerate, responsible and switched-on.

He's well-mannered, articulate and sexy.

Generous with his time, willing to help, one in a million.

And she was never giving in to the growing attraction between them or the feelings she had bubbling beneath the surface.

Chas came first, now and for ever.

She would be the model mum if it killed her.

'There's something else I wanted to talk to you about,' Riley said, not moving an inch. Maya was leaning so far back in her chair to give them some space that she was in serious danger of toppling backwards, chair and all.

'What's that?'

'Us.'

Maya clenched her jaw tight to prevent it from dropping open, her eyes darting frantically around for an escape.

She wasn't going to have this conversation.

Having fanciful dreams about Riley was one thing, having the guy sit there looking calm while wanting to discuss what she'd only thought to be in her imagination another.

'Uh—'

'Here you go, folks. Enjoy.' The waiter deposited their frosted glasses on the table, winked at her and sauntered away, giving her valuable seconds to think.

However, there was only one response to a bombshell

like the one Riley had just dropped and she hardened her heart, knowing it would hurt to deliver a line so patently untrue.

'We're friends,' she said, staring at the twinkling city lights over his right shoulder, unable to meet his steady stare. 'Just friends.'

She'd been wrong.

It didn't just hurt, it ached and throbbed like an old wound as the last small piece of hope she'd harboured in her heart curled up and died.

Hope that they could move past the scandal associated with Joe's death, past the old ties, and look to a future without hang-ups or gossip or possible whispers about Chas's mother and his uncle.

'We need to talk about this. This attraction between us…' Riley reached forward to take her hand but she snatched it away, knowing his touch would unravel her in a second. 'We need to be honest.'

Taking a steadying breath, she pushed her chair back and stood, knowing she had to end this here and now before he coerced her into saying more than she could allow. She couldn't fight him and her own feelings.

'You know I'm a straight-shooter. You want honesty? You've been an amazing support to me, not just the last few weeks but straight after Joe's death. You stood by me and I truly appreciate everything you've done. You're a great uncle and a wonderful friend. But that's all we can ever be. Friends.'

His eyes glittered with emotion, whether anger, confusion or something deeper she had no idea and she'd prefer to keep it that way. She didn't want to delve into her feelings, let alone his right now.

She didn't wait for his response. Head held high, she concentrated on the onerous task of putting one high-heeled foot in front of the other and walked out of the bar, managing to hold on to her dignity till she reached the black and gold bathroom next to the ballroom where she collapsed on to a plush ruby ottoman with the aplomb of a rag doll who'd had the stuffing ripped out of her.

Friends.

Nothing had to change between them. They could ignore the last part of their little chat tonight and go on as before.

Then why did she have a sinking feeling that the gleam she'd seen in his eyes before walking out of the bar held more than a hint of challenge?

CHAPTER NINE

RILEY WATCHED MAYA dancing with Brett Gould, her handsome boss, trying to dismiss the nasty niggle in his chest as heartburn from the rich Beef Wellington he'd had for dinner. However, he wasn't stupid. He couldn't confuse heartburn with jealousy and, at that moment, he knew he had a distinct case of the latter.

Logical? No.

Ridiculous? Yes.

Brett was happily married with two bouncing boys of his own and was the epitome of a loving family man, yet here Riley was, turning greener by the minute at the sight of Brett's hand splayed over Maya's back and the constant smiling chatter they kept up throughout the way-too-slow song.

How had he made such a mess of things? For a whiz in the boardroom, his communication skills sure went awry around Maya.

He'd never given much credence to Joe's off the cuff remarks, putting his brother's jibes down to his constant competitiveness since they'd been kids. But he was beginning to think that Joe hadn't been far off the mark when he'd said that a woman like Maya would never look twice at a dull workaholic like him.

It had been the final time they'd spoken, the night Joe had died, and the guilt that he'd contributed to his brother's death constantly weighed him down. Joe had made him so damn mad, telling him the only reason he'd gone after Maya was because he'd seen the way Riley had looked at her at this very event two years earlier.

Joe's casualness had sickened Riley and he'd done the only thing known to really hurt his brother, refusing to bail him out financially any more. Joe had turned nasty then, a torrent of abuse pouring forth. Most of it had centred around how much their parents had favoured Riley, how Joe had spent his life trying to beat him and how he hated being second best.

Riley had been stunned at the depth of Joe's animosity. Despite the urge to mollycoddle him as he had his whole life, Riley had stood firm. Joe had walked out after calling him a miserable old bastard and that had been the last time he'd seen his brother alive. The extent of Joe's gambling debts and the mess he'd left Maya and Chas in reinforced his guilt that if he'd given in to Joe that day, his brother would still be alive.

And Riley'd be exactly where he was right now: wanting the one woman he couldn't have.

Thankfully, the song ended and Maya slipped from Brett's arms, uncertainty flickering across her beautiful face as she scanned the perimeter of the dance floor.

The next dance was his.

She'd avoided him for most of the evening, flitting from one dance partner to another, telling him she had to network, and he'd tortured himself by imagining every smile, every glance she cast at her partners as meaningful.

Smart? No.

Stupid? You bet.

Just because he'd blundered into the sensitive topic of what he'd hoped was a burgeoning relationship between them with all the finesse of a lumbering elephant and Maya had harpooned him accordingly, it didn't mean she was at fault for making small talk with a bunch of work colleagues.

Besides, she may have thought she'd had the final word but she was wrong.

She wanted to stay friends for now? Fine.

As reticent as he may have been with women in the past, he wasn't a complete fool and, if he'd read the signs correctly, Maya was attracted to him.

Egotistical? No.

Wishful thinking? Oh yeah.

But, either way, he had no intention on giving up.

Striding through the crowd, he watched her fiddling with the sash at her slim waist, nibbling on her bottom lip, her eyes sweeping the room. She looked incredible, the sassy strapless dress hugging every delicious curve of her body, her blonde hair swept up in a sophisticated style which didn't detract from the heart-stopping face beneath.

He'd been gobsmacked the first minute she'd walked into the bar and, as she caught sight of him now, her eyes widening and her lips curving in a small nervous smile, the same overwhelming 'wow' factor slammed into him, rendering him dumbstruck.

'I really need to go after this dance,' she said, casting an almost frantic glance at the band as if willing them to play a quick song and be done with it. 'Tomorrow's a big day.'

Managing to unglue his tongue from the roof of his mouth long enough to reply, he said, 'Sure.'

She cast him a strange look, obviously expecting him to say more but instead he whisked her into his arms as the first strains of a waltz filled the room. Words he could botch, holding her close would be a cinch.

'I'm not very good at this,' she said, her posture rigid, her hand clasping his lightly as she averted her head to one side, determined not to make eye contact.

'Neither am I. Just sway in time to the music, it'll all be over before you know it.'

Her gaze snapped up to his and he silently cursed for letting that last bit slip. He hadn't meant to say it but, after seeing her so willing and pliant in the arms of her other dance partners in comparison to her stiff, unyielding body now, a streak of bitterness hammered home the fact that she didn't want to be this close to him.

'Don't do this, Riley.'

'What? Dance with a friend?'

He deliberately kept his voice devoid of inflection, not wanting her to misinterpret anything else. He'd bungled enough for one night. This dance was supposed to make up for that, to take a step in the right direction to re-cementing their friendship and, hopefully, towards more. Much more.

Her mouth relaxed out of its grim line at his response, along with some of her body's stiffness. 'Touché.'

'Look, how about we don't talk and just enjoy the dance?' That way, he couldn't say the wrong thing and mess up what little of the evening remained.

'Fine.'

Thankfully, the last of the residual tension left her body as she relaxed into his hold, her cheek resting lightly on his lapel as he guided them around the dance floor, wishing he could have her in his arms like this for ever.

Yes, they were friends but logic told him otherwise.

He respected her decision to keep him at arm's length but he didn't agree with it.

However, if Maya wanted him as her friend, it would just have to do.

For now.

Maya dashed into the powder room, needing a few seconds to steady her nerves before driving Riley home.

She'd known tonight would be tough and she'd been right, big time. Everywhere she'd turned people had asked how she was coping and was there anything they could do and what Material Girl's chances in the Cup tomorrow were. 'Fine, no and good' had become her stock-standard answer and, though she'd soon tired of the constant barrage, at least it had kept her away from Riley.

Not that it had helped. She'd felt his eyes on her everywhere she'd moved and, darn it, she'd liked it. In fact, she'd liked far too much about this evening: the way he looked, the way he stared at her with something bordering on need in his eyes and the way he made her feel when he'd spun her around the ballroom like Cinderella with Prince Charming.

She'd danced with many guys and had mentally convinced herself that dancing with Riley wouldn't be any different.

Yeah, right.

*Friends…friends…friends…*had echoed through her mind as they'd twirled between the other dancing couples. Try as she might, it had been difficult to remember her own rules when it felt as if his hand was burning a hole through the satin in the small of her back and his spicy aftershave had impregnated her smell receptors for ever.

And now she'd offered to give him a lift home out of politeness and her plans to beat a hasty retreat, the main reason why she'd brought her own car in the first place, had gone up in smoke.

As the door opened and a burst of giggling followed, she dashed into a cubicle, not wanting to make small talk with anyone else tonight. Many people had been genuine in their concern for her welfare but she'd also seen the sideways stares, the snide smirks when she'd danced with Riley—another reason why she'd kept her distance.

Those who knew her in racing circles liked and respected her but, unfortunately, many of Joe's shallow phoney friends were here too and she'd steered well clear of their plastic smiles and fake platitudes.

'Did you see her draped all over Joe's brother? Didn't take her long.'

Maya froze as a shrill voice drifted over the cubicle partition, hoping the cruel words weren't aimed at her and insanely jealous if they weren't.

'Yeah, she's a real piece of work. You know the only reason Joe looked twice at a plain Jane like her was because she got knocked up? Everyone knows it.'

Bile rolled in Maya's stomach and she braced herself against the cubicle wall, wishing she'd never come in here as the character assassination continued.

'Where's Joe's kid while she's here making a play for his brother? Some mother she must be.'

Fury surged through Maya's body and she blinked back tears, repressing the urge to fling open the door and pummel the two bitchy women till they couldn't speak any more.

'And all dolled up. It's pathetic when these horsy women try too hard. You can pick them a mile away with their broken fingernails and split ends.'

Maya found herself studying her nails unwittingly, noting several overhanging cuticles and a few cracks, which didn't help her anger.

'Oh, well. She can try all she likes but a man with Riley's class isn't going to look twice at a jumped-up trollop like her. He's only paying her attention for the kid. Wouldn't surprise me if he took the kid off her hands and raised him as a Bourke. Give the kid a fighting chance at having a decent life.'

'Too right. You ready to head back? My lippie's fixed.'

'Let's go.'

Maya waited till the door slammed before stepping out of the cubicle, the tears she'd been battling to subdue trickling down her face in slow, sad rivulets.

It couldn't be true.

Riley cared about her. He'd intimated as much tonight, wanting to talk about them. She'd been the one to head him off, to establish boundaries. Surely she hadn't miscued?

But what if those vile women were right?

What if the only reason he was getting in good with her was to get close to Chas before snatching him away?

It wasn't the first time she'd thought it. Back then she'd told him to stick his kind intentions but now she knew him. At least she thought she did.

He had money to burn while she had nothing, a fact he was all too aware of. If it came to a legal battle, she couldn't afford to fight him. Worse, her character wouldn't stand up to any probing investigations: she came from a broken home and was a single mother living in a hovel.

Hell.

Suddenly, his kind offer to look after Chas while giving her some much-needed time out took on a whole new meaning.

Grabbing a handful of tissue, she wadded it into a ball and dabbed at the tears now coursing down her cheeks.

She'd never listened to idle gossip before and now wasn't the time to start. However, as she made a valiant attempt to fix her make-up, she couldn't help but wonder if Riley was as good an actor as Joe had been and if his consideration didn't hide a more sinister motive.

CHAPTER TEN

'GO, GIRL! GO!'

Maya yelled at the top of her lungs, jumping up and down on the spot as the Melbourne Cup field rounded the final turn and headed into the straight.

'She's in prime position,' Riley said, his eyes glued to the horses through binoculars. 'Albert's riding her a treat. Has her coasting, not using the whip at all, looks like he's about to give her a gee-up and let her go.'

'I can't stand it!'

Maya's gaze flicked between the mare—which could provide her son with a decent education and financial security if she won—and the tall man in a designer suit standing next to her, his neck muscles rigid with excitement as he leaned forward in an effort to keep the horses in sight.

'She's moving up. Two hundred metres to go and she's cutting through a pack on the rails!'

'Oh!'

Maya gripped Riley's arm as everything seemed to slow down. The deafening yells of a hundred thousand punters cramming Flemington racecourse faded into the background and, like a movie stuck in slow motion, she watched Material Girl—the mare who wouldn't run unless Maya gave her a pre-race pat and a whisper of encouragement, the mare who had listened to her tales of woe about Joe while she'd groomed, the mare who had an uncanny ability to know when she was feeling down and would snuggle into her with a soft whinny—split through a bunch of horses on the inside of the track and hit the front.

'She's got it!' Riley yelled, dropping his binoculars and jumping up and down like a madman. 'Go, you good thing! Go!'

Time stood still as Material Girl flashed past the winning post, the deafening roar of cheering washing over Maya in a wave.

'She won. I can't believe it; she won!'

Maya and Riley turned to each other at the same instant and she leapt into his arms, wrapping her hands tightly around his neck as he smacked a whopping kiss on her lips.

It was a heat of the moment embrace that didn't mean a thing. However, Riley didn't move and Maya found herself relishing the feel of his strong lips against hers, lips which gentled and moved in a light, feathery skid across hers, teasing her to prolong the contact, to savour the moment.

And she did, without thought or reason.

She slid down his body, her soft chest pressed against a wall of hard muscle that had her itching to feel more, to feel it bare, to feel it all.

Desire slammed through her body, the strength of it taking her breath away. She'd never experienced anything like it before, this crazy need to know a guy in every intimate way.

With Joe she'd been naïve, innocent, a girl who'd never had a chance to date let alone know what it felt like to be with a man. She'd equated sex with love though the act itself had left her cold.

Yet here she was, pressing herself against Riley in wanton abandonment, wishing he'd kiss her properly with heat and passion while stripping her naked and making love to her.

Her eyes fluttered open as Riley broke the kiss and set her away from him, a stunned expression on his face.

'She's a champion,' he said, managing a rueful smile as he turned back to the track, effectively breaking the awkwardness of the moment and giving her a much-needed second or two to compose herself.

She'd kissed Riley.

Riley had kissed her.

Oh, no…

Okay, it hadn't exactly been the most romantic kiss and it hadn't been pre-planned but the minute his lips had touched hers, she'd lost her mind!

They were friends.

Friends exchanged impulsive, congratulatory smooches but their lip-lock had been more than that, she was certain of it.

Thankfully, Brett appeared by her side and she hugged

him, not surprised to see the sheen of tears in the owner and trainer's eyes.

'She did it. The Girl did it,' Brett said, clasping her hands and squeezing tight.

'She sure did,' Maya said, feeling truly happy for the first time in a long time.

Yes, the money would take a major load off her mind but there was more to it. Glancing around at the ecstatic connections of Material Girl—the other co-owners in the syndicate, Brett, the stable hands—she had a strong sense of belonging.

She was a part of all this and, though she'd never had a family of her own as such, surrounded by people who genuinely cared for her and who shared in the joy of today, it didn't matter.

'Congratulations, Brett.' Riley shook the other man's hand and Brett slapped him on the back.

'And thanks to you, mate. If you hadn't stepped in and helped us out, the Girl wouldn't have run today let alone won. Damn mare won't do anything without this little lady by her side.' Brett tweaked Maya's nose and she grinned, happy to join in the banter.

'And don't you forget it!'

They laughed, turning in unison towards the entrance to the mounting yard where Albert was standing in the stirrups, holding his whip aloft and pumping the air in a victory salute. Material Girl had her ears pricked and swung her head from side to side as if checking out the crowd and wondering what all the fuss was about.

'I'll never forget this day,' Maya said softly, grateful

for this little ray of sunshine in what had been a pretty dreary year so far.

'Me either.'

She looked up at Riley, expecting his gaze to be firmly fixed on the Girl. Instead, his blue eyes shone with excitement as he tipped up her chin with his index finger and stared directly at her.

'Friends, remember?' she blurted, suddenly over-whelmed by her erratic heartbeat, her deep-seated yearnings and the fervent glint in his eyes.

'I remember,' he said, a confident smile curving his lips and drawing her attention to them just when she needed to concentrate on forgetting how darn great they'd felt pressed against hers.

'Hey, Eddy! We did it!'

Maya turned in time to see Albert leap from the mare and land squarely on his feet, giving her two thumbs up in victory.

Her head swung back to Riley, torn between wanting to hear what he had to say and running to Albert.

'Go,' Riley said, giving her a gentle push in the jockey's direction. 'This is your day. Enjoy it.'

'Thanks.'

Smiling, she raced towards Albert and joined in a group hug with Brett and the jockey, who'd made an unerring judgement call yesterday when he'd said she had feelings for Riley, while photographers snapped away and journalists crowded around them thrusting microphones in their faces.

'Great ride, Al,' she said, high-fiving the grinning jockey while flashes continued to light up around them.

'Piece of cake.'

Albert dropped a quick peck on her cheek—the type of kiss she should've got from Riley but she was real glad she'd got more. 'I did it all, you know. The strapper didn't have the slightest influence in the greatest win in Melbourne Cup history ever.'

Maya rolled her eyes, slapped him playfully and turned to the mare, who almost meant as much to her as Chas.

'Who's a clever girl?' Maya murmured, stroking the mare's nose as she snuggled into her for a characteristic hug.

'You are,' Brett said, touching her on the arm while slipping the winner's shiny blue satin blanket over the Girl. 'That bonus we discussed before the race is all yours.'

'Thanks, boss,' she said, hoping she wouldn't blubber in front of Brett.

'Thank you for all your hard work. You deserve it.'

Brett winked and walked towards the throng of cameras, leaving her alone with the mare whose amazing endurance in running three thousand two hundred metres—and winning—had just earned her one hundred thousand dollars.

Money that would go a long way to making life easier for her son.

But what about her life?

After that kiss she'd shared with Riley, nothing in her life seemed clear or easy.

* * *

'Are you sure you'll be okay?'

Maya lingered in the hallway of Riley's million-dollar Docklands penthouse apartment, her gaze darting from Chas, playing with a new puzzle on the floor, to Riley, all but pushing her out the door.

'We'll be fine. It's only for one night. How much trouble do you think we boys can get into in that space of time?'

She saw Chas stuff a piece of soft puzzle into his mouth and look around for a toy chaser, his cherubic face split by a demonic grin.

'Plenty,' she said, knowing her son was in good hands with Riley yet unable to shrug off her paranoia.

She couldn't forget what those women had said in the powder room at the ball last week and, now that the time had come to leave Chas for the first time, her previous doubts flooded back.

Was Riley like Joe but a better actor?

Was his kindness a front for getting in good with her and Chas before he staged a coup and took Chas away from her?

The very idea seemed ludicrous, and she'd told herself that repeatedly since the ball, yet she'd been suckered once. Surely she'd grown up and wised up since?

Then what was her excuse for having these ridiculous feelings for Riley that wouldn't go away?

No matter how many times she berated herself for being stupid, for acting like a fool, for wishing for something that she'd never let happen, her insides twisted in knots every time he so much as looked her way.

Which was what this break was all about. Her first step towards putting some much-needed distance between them. He'd been there for her when she'd needed him the most but now it was time to step back, take stock and get her life back on track without the dependable shoulder of Riley Bourke to lean on whenever she needed it.

'It's not like you'll be miles away. You're staying up the road and I promise to call if anything dire happens, which it won't,' he added, seeing the flash of panic in her eyes. 'You just check into that hotel, spend hours in their day spa and do whatever you need to do to chill out, okay?'

'Okay.'

She hadn't wanted to touch a cent of her bonus from Material Girl's Cup win for herself but Riley had insisted, nagging her till she'd booked an overnight stay at one of Melbourne's swankiest hotels to shut him up. Now that the time had come, a small part of her was eternally grateful for his pushiness as she couldn't wait to relax for the first time in two years. The rest of her wanted to pick up her little boy from the floor and hang on to him for dear life.

'Good. Off you go, then.' Riley held open the door and did a funny bow to usher her out.

'Slave-driver,' she mumbled, rushing back into the lounge to give Chas one last kiss and cuddle before heading out the door.

'Have fun,' Riley said, enveloping her in a quick hug

before releasing her all too soon. 'And don't worry. We'll be fine.'

'Uh-huh.'

Despite Riley's reassurances, despite how close he'd grown to Chas and how capable he was, she took the sleek lift down to the ground floor with her heart plummeting along with the steel cage.

Riley was the perfect role model for Chas and he would've made a great father. Coupled with her burgeoning feelings, she could've had the family of her own that she'd always craved.

Instead, she had to turn her back on it all because of one tiny biological fact: Riley was Joe's brother and she wouldn't go there.

Friends, she could do. A strong, uncomplicated friendship that would benefit Chas and give her someone to share the load if needed.

Friends was good.

Friends was all they could ever be.

Maya lay back on a comfy chaise longue, every muscle in her body liquefied after a half hour soak in a mineral bath and an hour long Swedish massage that had her sighing with pleasure with every stroke.

This is the life, she thought as she sipped a refreshing ginger-infused honey tea and flicked through a stack of magazines. How long since she'd felt like this, as if the boulders of stress strung across her shoulders and weighing her down like some obscene necklace had been pulverised into nothing?

Try never.

Her whole life had consisted of tiptoeing around her mother or cleaning up after her and then she'd had more of the same with Joe.

Thinking of her mum, she realized she'd missed her monthly visit, courtesy of her torn ankle ligaments and then the Cup preparations had gone ballistic. No matter how hard it was to see her mum in a vegetative state most of the time, Maya tried never to miss a visit and was way overdue for one.

Though she wouldn't think about that now. The mere thought of seeing her mum's vacant stare, her listless face and her fidgeting hands had her neck muscles re-tightening.

Finishing the rest of the tea in three gulps, she flicked the pages of the latest *Flirt* issue, Melbourne's hippest magazine. However, rather than the action de-stressing her, she found her hands shaking and her blood pressure spiking as she stared at the half page picture, bold caption and accompanying article.

A FINE FILLY ON TO A WINNER?

Stockbroking whiz Riley Bourke congratulates Material Girl's strapper Maya Edison after the mare's stunning victory in the Melbourne Cup, the race that stops a nation. Riley, the brother of Ms Edison's deceased fiancé, Joe Bourke, had been seen squiring the lovely strapper at the Cup Eve Ball the night previously at the Palladium, and if a picture paints a thousand words we can safely say that the cosy couple are more than just friends.

A source confirmed that Riley Bourke has been seen around the Flemington stables where Ms Edison works on a regular basis, and is more than comfortable with Ms Edison's young son, who also happens to be his nephew.

Is Ms Edison keeping it all in the family? Stay tuned to the Flirt Alert to find out more.

Mortified, Maya closed her eyes, took a deep breath and reopened them, refocusing on the glossy photo of the post-race kiss she'd shared with Riley. The article was a load of trash but there was no arguing with the vivid image of the two of them plastered against each other, arms entwined, sharing what looked like a passionate kiss.

Everyone who saw that picture and read the article would believe she was a tart, just like the gossip-mongers had already been saying and, thanks to *Flirt*'s readership, that would be a lot of people.

Not that it bothered her. She knew the truth and it wasn't this trumped up piece of rubbish journalism designed to sell copies.

However, what horrified her most was that the article was exactly the type of mud she didn't want sticking to Chas and seeing the evidence of her growing feelings for Riley plastered across a national magazine was the wake-up call she needed.

No more impulsive displays of affection.

No more time spent together.

If Riley wanted to see Chas, she would set up a formal visiting system, through a lawyer if she had to, but the three of them would have to stop hanging out and doing the regular stuff that families did.

Riley wasn't her family and he never would be.

The sooner she started to believe it the better.

Flinging the magazine back on to the pile, she lay back and massaged her temples, knowing what she had to do, all too aware of how difficult it would be to carry out.

CHAPTER ELEVEN

RILEY PACED THE hospital corridor, passing the same tilted vending machine, the uncomfortable bright orange plastic chairs and the small TV on mute that he'd seen for the last ten minutes since he'd made the call to Maya.

Having rushed Chas to the Royal Children's Hospital an hour ago when the little tyke had been making a God-awful barking sound between a cough and a croak and couldn't seem to take a breath, he'd been dreading making the call to Maya.

Thankfully, he'd waited till the doctors had seen Chas, diagnosed him with a bout of croup and given him a shot of corticosteroid before calling, needing to reassure her that everything was okay.

As he'd anticipated, it hadn't worked. Though Maya hadn't freaked out over the phone, her tight voice, controlled sniffing and curt announcement that she'd be there in ten minutes told him she hadn't bought his reassurances for a second. Not that he could blame her.

Though the doc had explained that croup was a common occurrence in toddlers, some kind of virus of the voice box, he would never forget waking up to the sound of the little guy struggling for breath, trying to cry in fear but croaking instead.

It must've been something he'd done or not done. Some guys were cut out for the whole kid-rearing thing and it looked as if he wasn't one of them.

He adored Chas and wanted to give Maya as much help as he could but maybe this wasn't the way to go about it? Perhaps he should be the type of uncle who sent birthday cards with money, made the occasional phone call and that was all?

It didn't matter what he thought. He had a feeling Maya wouldn't let him near Chas after this episode anyway.

At that moment Maya burst through the swinging doors at the end of the corridor and sprinted towards him, blonde curls streaming behind her, bright blue hooded top slipping off one shoulder, short denim skirt restricting her movements and mismatched shoes.

'Where is he?' she demanded, skidding to a halt in front of him and fixing him with a mistrustful glare. 'I want to see him now!'

He reached out a placatory hand before thinking better of it and letting his arm drop to his side. 'He's sleeping. The doctor said he'll be fine.'

He didn't add that the doc had also said that if he hadn't acted so quickly things could've been a lot worse for Chas.

'Take me to him.' She grabbed his arm in a vice-like grip and started marching towards the nurse's station. 'Now.'

Riley led her to a small room opposite the lift and pointed through the window. 'He's in there.'

He took a step towards the door with her but she whirled on him like a protective lioness. 'You wait here,' she said, her voice a low growl, a perfect fit for his analogy, and he nodded, wanting to give her space but fighting the urge to watch over her too.

Damn, backing away would be tough. Not just because he'd miss the little guy but because he'd miss Maya so much too. He'd grown used to being needed, had enjoyed playing the hero—feelings he'd never experienced in the frenetic business world he usually called home.

As great as seeing the Girl win the Cup had been, the minute the mare had flashed past the finishing post, he'd known his time with Maya and Chas had come to an end.

And he knew he wanted more. More than the tentative friendship she was offering, more than the occasional platonic peck.

Stupidly, he'd attributed her reticence to guilt; he was Joe's brother, Joe was dead and she didn't deserve to be happy or something along those lines.

Then he'd had a wake-up call. What if she just didn't feel the same way he did? Sure, there was a sizzle of underlying attraction between them but that could be explained away as sheer physical chemistry.

She hadn't given him any indication that their relationship went beyond friendship, even though he'd tried to read more into that impulsive kiss after her protégée had won the Cup than there was. Unfortunately, whichever way he looked at it, he was flogging a dead horse—so to speak.

Maya didn't have feelings for him, he had feelings for Maya. A simple equation for a smart guy like him. It was the solution he didn't like.

He watched Maya bend over Chas and kiss the little boy on his forehead, straightening the bedclothes and hovering over him like an angel as a fist squeezed his heart, causing an ache to spread through his chest.

Maya and Chas needed him.

They were a part of his world now, a major part, a part he wanted to nurture and develop into something warm and special.

Not any more.

Shaking his head, he turned away from the poignant scene of mother and son and headed for the drinks machine, finding a lukewarm cup of putrid coffee better than mulling over his depressing thoughts.

He'd barely taken a sip when Maya joined him and pointed to a nearby empty alcove.

'Coffee?'

'No, thanks.' She dropped into a plastic chair and ran a hand through her hair, her delicate fingers tangling in the curls before she yanked her hand free and clasped it with the other one as if to still it.

'What happened?'

He sat next to her, taking care not to touch her. Her

body language screamed 'hands off' and by the feral gleam in her eye, she'd probably take a swing at him.

'I don't know. One minute he was sleeping peacefully, the next he couldn't breathe.'

'Did you take him into the bathroom immediately and turn on the shower? Steam is the best thing for croup.'

He shook his head, feeling more inadequate by the minute. For a guy who could handle million dollars' worth of stock, he knew diddly-squat when it came to kids.

'No. I didn't know what was going on so I brought him here ASAP.'

Her hands clasped so tight, her knuckles turned white. 'Why didn't you ring me immediately?'

'Because I didn't have time to think. I did what I thought was right at the time and that was to get medical attention. You weren't there, you didn't hear him struggling for breath…' He trailed off, knowing it was the wrong thing to say the minute all colour drained from her pale face.

However, rather than berate him for his lack of sensitivity, she said in a soft, wavering voice, 'No, I wasn't there.'

Her bottom lip quivered and, before he could blink, she burst into tears, loud, noisy sobs that shook her body and had him hauling her into his arms to offer what little comfort he could.

'This is my fault. I should never have left him,' she sobbed, clutching his shirt and raising a tear-streaked face to look up at him.

If he hadn't suffered a major blow several minutes

earlier when he'd realised what he had to give up, the bereft, guilt-ridden expression in her shimmering eyes now would've done the trick.

'Hey, don't say stuff like that. The doc said most kids get a bout of croup in their lives and there's nothing you can do. It's just one of those things.'

Funny, he could say the words to placate a distraught Maya but he didn't believe them himself. This wasn't her fault, it was his and it was about time he took the fall.

'Besides, if anyone's to blame it's me. Chas was in my care and I let him down. I didn't know about the shower stuff; maybe I could've prevented the attack from getting worse.'

He half expected her to rebuff him, to say that none of this was anyone's fault, but she didn't. Instead, she pulled away from him and wiped away her tears with the back of her hand, her characteristic defiance reasserting itself as she tilted her chin up to look him in the eye.

'Why don't you go home? I'm here now.'

'I'd like to stay,' he said, hating the gulf that had opened up between them but knowing it was necessary. He had to disengage from their family unit and, as much as it pained him, now was as good a time as any.

'I'd like you to go.'

She met his gaze unflinchingly, the sheen of tears adding to the richness of her green irises and not detracting from her beauty one iota. Even with no make up, dark rings circling her eyes, a red nose from crying and tear streaks down her cheeks, she was still the most beautiful woman he'd ever seen.

'Call me if you need me,' he said, recognising the irony in his words.

She'd said the same thing to him less than twelve hours earlier when she'd left Chas in his care, not expecting him to do it.

She sent him a curt nod and turned away, effectively dismissing him. This time he knew she had no intention of calling on him for help no matter how dire things were.

Hating the helpless feeling that consumed him, he strode down the corridor, reaching the far door when her voice halted him.

'Riley?'

He stopped and swivelled on his heel to face her, hoping she'd call him back but knowing the odds weren't stacked in his favour. 'Yeah?'

'Thanks.'

He smiled, resisting the urge to run back down the corridor and sweep her into his arms. Instead, he raised his hand in a farewell salute but she'd already turned away and headed back into Chas's room.

Maya ran the gamut of emotions while Chas slept peacefully in his hospital bed. Disappointment and doubt in herself and her abilities as a mother, anger and disillusionment that Riley could be just as irresponsible and useless as his brother. The emotions bounced around her brain till she slumped down in an uncomfortable plastic chair and dropped her head in her hands.

She should never have left Chas with Riley.

Bad move.

What kind of mother was she to leave her precious son while she went swanning off for some self-indulgence? A rotten one, that was for sure and way too much like her own irresponsible mum for comfort.

Her mum hadn't cared when she'd left Maya alone in their dreary house, in their appalling neighbourhood, in the middle of the night, to go out for more alcohol. Maya had hated those nights, which had happened all too frequently, when she'd hear the clink of empty bottles and the muttered curses as her mum searched for money and stumbled against furniture in her haste to make it to the local bottle shop before closing.

Her first recollection of such a night was when she'd been six and she'd shivered under a threadbare blanket in the dead of winter, petrified by the branches slamming against her window in the gale outside, the old weatherboard house creaking around her ears, silent tears pouring down her face as she prayed for her mummy to come back.

Her prayers had been answered but, unfortunately, her mum was never any use when she'd come back from her night jaunts.

'Miss Edison?'

Maya jumped at the light touch on her shoulder and carefully schooled her face into a semblance of normality before looking up at the young nurse standing over her.

'Why don't you go home? Your son is fine and will sleep till the morning. You could take him home now if you wanted but we've got the extra bed for the night, a rarity in this place, so why don't you let him rest and pick him up first thing?'

'No, I'd rather stay.' Maya glanced at her watch, having lost track of time since Riley's midnight phone call. 'Chas is an early riser and he'll be up in a few hours.'

The nurse fiddled with the fob chain attached to a watch pinned to her pocket, a slight frown between her plucked eyebrows. 'You sure? If you don't mind me saying, you look worn out. Maybe a few hours sleep at home is exactly what the doctor ordered.'

The nurse grinned at her pun and Maya mustered a weak smile in return. 'Thanks, but I'm fine.'

The nurse hovered before shrugging. 'Okay, but if you want a blanket, they're in that supply cupboard over there.'

'Great.'

Maya kept the smile on her face till the nurse turned her back, slumping into the hard plastic once she'd disappeared.

Okay, maybe she was being a tad tough on herself. She was nothing like her mother and never would be. Life was about choices, like not touching alcohol and making sure the slightest whiff of scandal didn't touch her child.

It was sheer bad luck that Chas had fallen ill the one night she'd been away from him since his birth. It could've happened at any time and had nothing to do with Riley's competence as a carer either, even if she'd treated him otherwise.

She'd been so darn mad at him that she'd pushed him away when he was probably just as concerned about Chas as her. Her anger that he could be like Joe—totally and utterly useless when it came to child-rearing—had tainted her view of the situation and she'd reacted accordingly. Stupid, irrational and unfair. But then had she been anything but around Riley since Joe's death?

In some weird way, she'd made him pay for her own shame at being attracted to him. Whenever he'd looked at her or smiled at her or had just been there for her, she'd been reminded of how wrong it was to like him, to want him in a way that had nothing to do with friendship.

He was Joe's brother and no amount of dreaming or yearning for the impossible could change that.

It was just plain wrong to love him.

Who said anything about love?

Sighing, she closed her eyes and leaned her head back against the wall. She'd tried ignoring her feelings, she'd tried the friendship thing, and she'd tried her best to deny something she'd subconsciously known for a while now.

She loved Riley.

She loved how he cared for Chas, she loved how he pitched in and helped her whenever she needed it, but most of all she loved how he made her feel: like a woman—a beautiful, desirable woman. Joe had called her a dirty scruffy tomboy that night he drove off and wrapped his car around a pole.

The night he'd told her the real reason he'd ever looked her way in the first place—the only reason—and it brought tears of disgust to her eyes just thinking about it.

She'd been wrong to ever doubt Riley's capabilities

in caring for Chas or his intentions. Riley was nothing like Joe. They were poles apart.

And now it was too late.

Her love for Riley would stay a secret for the sake of her child, locked away where the gossips and scandal sheets couldn't defile it or use it against Chas.

Come tomorrow, she needed to make some changes, starting with distancing herself from Riley once and for all.

CHAPTER TWELVE

STAYING AWAY FROM Maya and Chas over the weekend almost killed Riley.

He checked the stock markets, went for a bike ride, played eighteen holes of very bad golf and grouched around the rest of the time feeling at a complete loss. Maya had been curt on the phone when he'd rung to enquire after Chas on the Saturday morning, not that he could reproach her.

She blamed him for what had happened with Chas; he blamed himself too. Ironically, it had taken the little guy scaring him to death to make him re-evaluate what the hell he was doing.

Since Joe's death, he'd been overcompensating in a big way, trying to be super-uncle, and it was time to stop. Yes, he could be an uncle to Chas, but from a distance—much safer that way. For all of them.

Which brought him to the main reason he now stood outside the main stable door on a chilly Monday morning, waiting for Maya to take a tea break so they could talk. Or, more accurately, so that he could say goodbye.

Blowing on his hands, he rubbed them together and cast malevolent glances at the dark clouds scudding across the sky. A fitting backdrop considering his bad mood. Usually he didn't mind the four-seasons-in-a-day Melbourne weather. Today, like everything else, it annoyed the hell out of him. Sydney would be a welcome change after this.

As Maya exited the stable, her curls tied back in a loose ponytail hanging halfway down her back, a fuzzy pink beanie on her head and a bulky blue plaid coat which belonged on a lumberjack rather than a gorgeous woman, he knew that Melbourne had a lot more going for it than its northern counterpart.

Maya lived in Melbourne—*which is exactly why you're going to Sydney.*

He blinked and focused his attention on getting through this farewell without making a total hash of it like he usually did when he got within two feet of this woman.

'You're up early,' she said, strolling up to him with a wary expression on her face. 'When you said you'd come by, I expected it to be at a decent hour. Like nine.'

'Thanks to my stint as stable-boy-wonder, I'm up with the birds these days.' He smiled, trying to lighten the moment, to broach the distance that had opened up between them since the hospital.

It didn't work.

'What did you want to talk about?'

Short, abrupt, cool. No small talk, no pleasantries and none of the vivacity that usually made her green eyes sparkle with life.

She'd changed and there had to be more behind it than Chas's croup and his part in it. It was as if shutters had come down, blanking out any sign of life, of emotion and, though he'd come to say goodbye, it scared him. He'd never seen her this lifeless, this introverted, and he struggled with the urge to throw his departure plans to the wind and stick around to make sure she'd be all right.

However, common sense won out and he knew that hanging around hoping for a miracle wasn't a wise move.

'I came to say goodbye,' he said, somewhat mollified when her eyes widened in shock before the tell-tale cool slid quickly into place again.

'Business?'

He managed a tight grin, wondering if she even cared. By her fidgeting hands and shuffling feet, it looked as if she couldn't wait to get rid of him.

'Yeah, you know me, business as usual. I haven't been into the office for a while and I miss it. Time to get back up into the saddle, so to speak. New deals, new challenges.'

If she'd asked, What deals? What challenges? he might've thought she cared.

She didn't ask.

'Are you going to say goodbye to Chas?'

'Uh-huh. I thought I'd head up to the house after this if that's okay with you?'

Her lips compressed into the thin, hard line he hated so much, the line that had vanished from her mouth in the amazing weeks he'd spent with her and Chas, growing closer, playing at happy families.

But it had been just that—*playing*. Time to pick up his bat and ball and go home, a loser. Something that didn't sit well with him, considering he'd always been a winner in his career.

'Sure.'

Maya thrust her hands into her pockets, hunching her shoulders and adding to the air of vulnerability that hung around her like a dark cloud. 'He'll miss you.'

He leaned forward, not sure if he'd heard correctly and wishing for the impossible, that she might say, I'll miss you.

It didn't happen.

Silently cursing himself for being a fool, he rummaged around in his coat pocket with icy fingers and pulled out his parting gift for Chas, the only good thing he could do for his nephew, the only thing he couldn't botch up.

'Here, this is for Chas. I wanted to do something for his future and I think this should help.'

He handed her the cheque, knowing he should've said how much he loved the little guy, how much he valued the precious time he'd spent with him, with both of them, but the words stuck in his throat. There was a reason he was so damn good in the business arena; he could deal with cold, hard facts. It was this nebulous emotion thing he had no way of controlling and he hated it.

Maya stared at the cheque. She didn't say a word as she looked at it, flicked her gaze up at him and back again, her face entirely blank.

'I'll send more on his birthdays and Christmas and if you ever need any more, just ask. Use it for his education or whatever.' He babbled on and on, desperate to fill the growing silence, wishing she'd say something, anything, before he turned on his heel and walked out of her life.

Finally she closed her mouth and lifted her eyes to his, green fire flashing like tiny lightning bolts. 'His education? Why? So he can go to some fancy private school and become an unfeeling, rich know-it-all who would rather buy a kid's affection than be there to give him the real thing?'

'Listen—'

'Thanks but no thanks. I've already told you what I think of your money.'

She tore the cheque into small pieces as she spoke, short, sharp, vicious rips of paper punctuating every word.

'It's not like that,' he said, not surprised by her reaction in the slightest.

Initially, when he'd made up his mind to leave, he'd thought she'd react like this, had counted on it. What better way to distance himself from the situation than to deliberately offer her money?

However, a small part of him had wished that after all they'd been through lately, she would understand where he was coming from, would give him the benefit of the doubt that he really loved Chas enough to want to give him the world and then some.

'You want to know what it's like?' She took a step towards him, her signature rose essence enveloping him in a welcome fog, drawing him physically closer while his mind took a step back and said stop!

'I'll tell you what it's like! You come into our lives playing knight in shining armour, boosting your own ego and making yourself feel so darn good for helping a couple of charity cases like us. Riley to the rescue. Riley the responsible one. Riley the do-gooder. You make Chas love you, you make me l—like you and then you waltz right out again, thinking a couple of hundred thousand can buy us off? Well, this is what I think of your generous attempt to buy my son's affection.'

He stood rooted to the spot as she tugged roughly on his pocket and stuffed the remnants of paper into it, a parody of a similar action she'd made towards him eons ago.

'There. Seem familiar? Hope that helps you sleep at night,' she said, sending him a scathing look while tears shimmered in her eyes. 'See you round, Riley Bourke.'

She stalked back into the stables, dragging the huge wooden door shut behind her with a loud bang, leaving him alone in the yard, the distant sound of horse's hooves thundering around the track not succeeding in drowning out the self-admonition 'stupid, stupid, stupid' ringing in his ears.

Maya stomped into the nearest empty stall and burst into tears, kicking at the fresh hay and glad there were no cats around.

She should've been furious that Riley had given her so much money.

She should've been happy that he'd made her life easier by putting some much needed distance between them—exactly what she'd intended on doing anyway.

Instead she shed tears of regret and bone-deep sorrow that the man she loved would walk away thinking she hated him.

Nothing could be further from the truth.

Sure, she'd seen red when she'd first looked at the cheque and had spouted all that stuff at him about being bought but her anger had been hollow. It was the shock of his impending departure that had made her lose it and not the staggering amount of money he'd given her.

'Hey, Eddy. What's all the blubbering about?'

Albert stuck his head over the stall door, his characteristic grin absent and a frown in its place.

'Go away,' she said, sniffling into a scrunched up tissue that had seen better days. 'Can't a girl have a bout of hay fever without getting the third degree?'

'Hay fever. Uh-huh.' Albert unlatched the door and stepped into the stall, his gaze moving from the messy hay at her feet to her face, which must look a fright considering she was cold, tired and upset. 'If you ask me, your sudden allergy has something to do with the guy I just saw heading towards the main house like a pack of stampeding brumbies were on his tail.'

'Who asked you? Maybe I'm allergic to short guys who go around poking their nose into other people's business?'

She folded her arms and glared at him, knowing her crack about his height should distract him. Albert loved poking fun at himself but hated anyone else mentioning his stature.

To her chagrin, he burst out laughing. 'Nice try. However, I find the subject of your love life much more riveting than giving you a dressing down for that nasty remark about me being vertically challenged.'

She managed a watery smile despite the empty feeling spreading through her body like a slow-travelling poison. Trust Albert to try to cheer her up even after she'd insulted him.

'I don't have a love life' she said, sinking on to a bale of hay and pointing to another for him to take a seat. 'And haven't we had this conversation before?'

Albert shook his head and spoke slowly, as if to a child. 'Listen up, baby cakes. Time to wake up and smell the manure. The guy's smitten, he'll do right by you and the brat.'

'You don't understand,' she said, another wan smile poking through at being called baby cakes.

'Then explain it to me.'

Weariness settled over her like a blanket and she rubbed a hand over her eyes, wanting to go home, hide under the covers and not come out for a week. Totally wishful thinking considering she hadn't had a full night's sleep since Chas's birth.

'What's there to explain? There's nothing going on between Riley and me and there never will be. I won't let Chas face that sort of scandal.'

Albert opened his mouth to respond but she rushed on, determined to put an end to this conversation.

'And there will be scandal, no doubt about it. People are already talking. I've been subjected to their vile conjecture at the funeral, at the Ball and in the media. I won't have my child grow up having to put up with that sort of insinuation.'

'I didn't realise it was that bad,' Albert said, all sign of teasing wiped off his face.

'It is. Now, if you don't mind, I have work to do.'

Plus several houses to see with a smarmy estate agent afterwards and a cranky child who'd become clingy since the bout of croup to drag along. There was only so much she could take and, right now, she'd reached the end of her tether.

She jumped off the bale and dusted off her butt, eager to get through the next few hours by burying herself in her job, the only thing that took her mind off her troubles. It had worked before and she'd make sure it worked again.

'But we haven't really talked. I haven't given you any of my helpful advice.'

Pausing at the stall door, she fixed Albert with a sad stare. 'There's nothing you can say. Riley walked away and it's a good thing. Maybe not for Chas but it is for me. It has to be this way for all our sakes.'

Now, if only she could believe it.

Riley had been a fool.

For a smart guy who had never quit anything in his life, he'd walked away from the best thing that had ever happened to him and for what?

Because he'd messed up that one time with Chas? Because Maya didn't want him as more than a friend?

He could learn to be a better uncle. Plenty of guys raised kids every day, guys less capable and driven than him. It wouldn't be a walk in the park, but then being an older brother to Joe hadn't been easy either and he'd practically raised him.

Maybe he did have what it took to care for a kid, to be more than just a once-a-year-visit type of guy, especially for a kid he loved to bits? And maybe Maya would see that his affection was real and he wasn't trying to buy anybody.

He'd gone back to the stable to tell her as much and he'd caught the tail-end of a conversation.

Riley walked away and it's a good thing.

It wasn't the phrase so much that echoed through his head but the way she'd said it, as if her heart was breaking because of it.

But that couldn't be true? That would mean she cared more than she'd let on and, if she cared, maybe there was a possibility of more?

If there was the slightest chance of anything beyond friendship developing between them, he had to make amends, had to make her see that it did not have to be this way for 'all our sakes'.

But how?

Glancing towards the main house, he saw Chas tottering on unsteady legs, chasing Brett's two older boys, an ear-splitting grin on his chubby face.

Suddenly it hit him. The answer to everything: a way

to make things right for all of them, a way to convince Maya how much Chas meant to him and, possibly, a way to explore what lay unsaid between them.

Slipping his mobile from his pocket, he punched in the number for Matt Byrne. He needed some papers drawn up. Fast.

CHAPTER THIRTEEN

MAYA SANK ON to the sagging sofa, shifting around to avoid the nasty springs digging into her butt, and cradled a steaming mug of cocoa in her hands, deriving small comfort from its warmth.

After her disastrous morning, she'd trudged around half of inner Melbourne checking out houses and not finding anything. Not that she'd been paying particular attention to any of them considering her mind kept wandering to her confrontation with Riley and how terrible she felt because of it.

Thankfully, Chas had gone down like an angel tonight and she'd had a half hour soak in the tub—ignoring her recurring thoughts about Riley, where he was and what he was doing—followed by a healthy wedge of leftover pizza and a caramel ice cream chaser.

Comfort food was a great distraction. Unfortunately, it hadn't worked and she hoped the cocoa would do the trick and help her drift off into uninterrupted sleep.

As if.

She drained the last of the cocoa and padded towards

the kitchen, stopping dead at the faintest knock on the front door. No way. It must've been the rattle-trap steel security door banging in the wind, for no visitors came knocking at her door, let alone at ten p.m.

Except one and he'd gone back to his cushy job.

She held her breath and stared at the door, waiting. Again, the softest of knocks and she hurried to it, torn between an instant surge of hope and wanting to clobber the insensitive clod for turning up now.

Pulling her robe tight, she opened the door a fraction.

'I'm sorry for turning up so late but I needed to see you. It's important.'

She glared at the insensitive clod, her heart doing a betraying somersault of joy, and opened the door reluctantly.

'I don't know what you're doing here. I thought everything had already been said.'

She stood back to let Riley in, refusing to acknowledge how incredible he looked in all black: black jeans, black T-shirt and black leather jacket, which looked buttery soft. At least the logical part of her brain refused to acknowledge it. The rest of her had a hard time trying not to drool.

'That's why I'm here. The wrong things were said and it's time those mistakes were rectified.' He smiled at her, the same sexy smile that had her heart beating way too fast as always and sent her scurrying to the furthest chair away from him, sitting on the sofa. She hoped a wayward spring stuck him right where it hurt the most.

'I'm tired, Riley. I don't want to rehash anything or discuss any mistakes. Let's agree to move on and leave it at that?'

'No.'

She raised an eyebrow, surprised at the force behind that one small word. He always spoke to her in a kind, gentle manner, as if he thought she would break.

'Yes.'

She tilted her head and tried to stare him down, not willing to give an inch. They were finished and his being here was futile. Not to mention he'd probably robbed her of any chance she had of sleeping thanks to his impromptu visit and, for that alone, she could kill him.

'I have something to show you.'

He pulled a thick folded wad of paper from his jacket pocket and made to hand it across to her before thinking better of it.

'Let me guess. It's the deed to the stables and another cheque,' she said, bitterness scouring her words.

He didn't buy into her angst. 'No, it's proof that I'm not trying to buy my way into Chas's heart. I love the little guy and I want to show you both just how much.'

Her curiosity piqued, she reached for the paper he now held out to her and unfolded it, shocked to her soul when her eyes lit on the first word in bold print.

'*Ownership?* You're giving Chas your apartment? Are you mad?'

Riley took a deep breath, knowing the next few minutes would make or break the tenuous chance Maya had granted him in even hearing him out.

'This isn't as crazy as you think. Chas and I have bonded over the last few months and I think it would be good to cement that, to help the little guy grow up with some stability, and having a home of his own will do that. I love him and I'll do my best to make sure he knows it too.'

She shook her head, blonde curls falling around her face in riotous confusion, her eyes wide and sad as he rushed on. 'I know you think I'm lousy at caring for him after the croup incident, but this is a chance to prove how much I care. Will you give me that chance?'

He came to an abrupt stop, hating how desperate he sounded. He'd delivered pitches around the world, he'd brokered deals worth millions and he would never have got half as far if he'd sounded like this.

'I don't believe this,' she said, her gaze flicking to the papers once more as if she couldn't comprehend what she was seeing, before she threw the papers on the coffee table and dropped her head in her hands.

'Maya!' He rushed to her side, hating the defeated posture, the despair he'd glimpsed in her eyes before she'd dropped her head.

He'd done this to her.

With his carefully rehearsed, well thought out, foolproof plan to show her how much he cared, he'd hurt her. Even when he'd been so careful not to scare her with his hopes for the future, his hopes that they could be more than just friends.

He knew how much she loved Chas, knew she'd do anything for her child, and he'd counted on it, hoping she'd see this as a genuine gesture from the heart. This wasn't like offering money; it was a solid gift, something Chas would have for ever if he wanted. Having a real home for her and Chas would be a step in the right direction and, given time, he'd hoped she'd let him back into their lives.

Fool! Right now, with her hair hiding her face but her body shaking, she probably hated him and there wasn't one damn thing he could do about it.

He was all out of options.

'Maya? I'm sorry.' He touched her shoulder, trying to comfort. A small piece of his soul shrivelled up and died when she flinched away from him.

She finally raised her head and he was surprised to see resignation in her eyes rather than tears.

'Don't be. I can see how much you care about Chas and that means a lot. It really does. You're a great guy with the best of intentions and I know you're trying to do the right thing for your nephew but he's my son. *My son.* I want to provide for him. I want to find us a house, to build us a home together. And, as grand a gesture as this is, my answer is no.'

She stood up abruptly and almost tripped over the ownership papers in her haste to leave the room.

He tried one last desperate plea to make her see sense. 'This isn't just about Chas and I think you know it.'

His heart leaped with hope as she stopped at the doorway and sent him a look of such longing, such need, that it took his breath away.

'My answer is still no,' she whispered, her gaze telling him more than her words ever could before she turned away and left him to let himself out.

* * *

'You've picked a good time to visit. Jill's having one of her better days,' the occupational therapist said as Maya entered the Edgewater special accommodation facility that had housed her mother for the last three years.

Ironic that once Maya had been relieved of caring for her mother another burden had come along shortly after in the form of Joe Bourke. Though she was better off than most. She had a beautiful healthy son, a job she enjoyed and, thanks to that job, enough money to keep the wolves from the door for a while.

She was a survivor. Always had been, always would be. As for the happily ever after she'd once dreamed of as a teenager, spending hours envisaging a better future while cleaning up her mum's vomit or fetching aspirins, it wasn't to be. Happy endings weren't part of the plan for the Edison women apparently.

Maya thanked the occupational therapist and headed to her mum's room, the last at the end of a long corridor. The scent of wisteria filled the air, a lovely fresh fragrance which complemented the pale lemon walls and duck-egg blue carpet. She'd been impressed with this place on sight and didn't mind paying the extra few hundred a month for her mum to stay here.

Feeling increasingly guilty that she'd missed last month's visit, Maya knocked softly on the door and pushed it open, praying that this visit would be easier than the last few when her mum had alternated between not knowing her and drifting into the past.

'Hi Mum, it's me.' She poked her head around the door, stunned by the sight that greeted her.

'Come in, my darling girl.'

The OT hadn't been wrong when she'd said her
mum was having a good day. Apart from the fact
she'd actually recognised Maya for the first time in
months, she sat on a small sofa near the window,
dressed in a carnation-pink leisure suit with her face
made up and faded blonde hair arranged in a loose
bun on top of her head. She looked lovely and exactly
how Maya remembered her on her few 'good' days
growing up.

'You look great, Mum.'

Maya smiled, crossed the room and planted a kiss on
her mum's lined cheek, the skin way too thin and papery
for a woman in her late forties, alcohol having drained
more than her mum's brain cells.

'Thanks, sweetheart. How are you?'

'Fine.'

Okay, so that was stretching the truth. She hadn't
slept a wink last night after Riley's impromptu visit and,
with the growing ache in the vicinity of her heart, she
doubted she'd get much sleep for the next year.

'You look tired. Here, come sit next to me.'

Her mum patted the cushion next to her and Maya
sat, knowing she must look a fright if her mum had
picked up on how exhausted she was.

'Do you know what I've been doing today?'

Maya stared at her mum, blue eyes bright, an
animated look on her face. She stifled the edge of bitterness that came with the wish that her mum could
be like this all the time. She had to shrug off her de-

pression, be grateful for small mercies, and if today was a good day for her mum, she needed to make the most of it.

'What's that?'

'Writing my memoirs!'

Her mum reached for a tiny green and purple spotted notebook tucked into the sofa and caressed the cover lovingly as if she'd written the next *New York Times* bestseller.

'Wow, that's great,' Maya said, though a shiver of apprehension skittered down her spine.

Maybe it wasn't such a great idea that her mum spent her time reminiscing about the past considering the pain she must have been in to have had to drown her sorrows most days.

'It's part of our memory training. That lovely occupational therapist said it would stimulate our brains.'

'Sounds interesting.'

Maya kept her answers brief and non-committal, expecting her mum to revert to her usual taciturn self any second. Besides, even if her mum wanted to delve into the past, she certainly didn't. She may be a lot of things but a glutton for punishment wasn't one of them.

'I lied to you about your father.'

Maya stiffened and glanced at her mum's face, wondering if this was the start of her wanderings. However, her mum's eyes hadn't lost the spark of intelligence that signalled lucidity and Maya held her breath, wondering what deep, dark secret would be revealed. She'd harassed her mum for so long when she was growing up, pestering her about who her father was, why he wasn't around, did he love her, why had he left them.

Her mum had ignored her at first, before finally giving her a few snippets which Maya had taken and wound into a brilliant fairy tale. She'd envisaged her father as some sort of heroic nomad, travelling the world working with poor children who needed him more than she did. This was the only reason that made sense, which gave her some comfort at being abandoned, before she had hit her teens and blamed her mother for everything.

She'd once accused her mum of driving her father away with her drinking. Maya had hated her for it. Her mum hadn't cared at the time. She'd coped by going on one of her worst blinders on record, succeeding in wiping herself out for twenty-four hours straight.

Just another day in the Edison household.

'We don't have to talk about this,' Maya said, sending the little polka-dot book the evil eye.

'Yes, we do, my girl.'

To her surprise, her mum reached out and took hold of her hand, the first time she'd instigated physical contact in years.

'Your father wasn't a philanthropist or a do-gooder or a man who spent his life helping others. He was a bum, a drifter who couldn't commit to anything, who couldn't last at a job more than a few months. He gambled, he smoked, he played around on me and he drank. A lot.'

Her mum's steady gaze flickered and she glanced away but not before Maya saw the agonising pain.

'He was the one who started me drinking. It was the only thing we had in common towards the end and I joined in, hoping he'd love me, love us…'

'Mum, don't.'

Maya squeezed her mum's hand, hating her devastated expression. So her father hadn't been the superhero she'd built him up to be in her imagination? So what? She was a big girl now and she'd given up believing in fairy tales a long time ago.

'I have to tell you. You'll understand why in the end.' Her mum took a deep breath, blinked rapidly several times and continued. 'You were such a good little girl, the perfect daughter, always looking after me. He left when you were three years old after I kicked him out for belting you one day. You'd knocked over his beer can and he lashed out, going ballistic, and I knew in that second that I'd made a horrible mistake in staying with him.' Tears filled her eyes and trickled down her cheeks. 'I put up with a lot but the minute he laid a finger on you, I could've killed him. So I kicked him out before I did anything that drastic.'

'My God,' Maya murmured, more traumatised by how rough her mum had had it than by any memories. 'Then why did you build him up to be some kind of hero?'

Her mum swiped at her tears, her eyes clearer than ever. 'Because you needed him to be. Because I was such a failure as a mother, because I took the easy way out and drowned my sorrows rather than facing up to the mess I'd made of both our lives, because I wanted you to think that I wasn't always such a loser, that a prince-like man could go for a pathetic woman like me. But, most of all, to give you the self-esteem that I never had, the self-esteem which would stop you from making the wrong choice like I did.'

Maya's heartbeat sped up and she broke into a cold sweat. It couldn't be genetic, surely? She'd blamed her own lack of self-esteem for taking up with Joe in the first place and believing his smooth lies. And her mum had tried to avoid this very situation by telling her a bunch of lies about her loser dad? How ironic.

'You did the best you could, Mum. You tried to protect me and that's what counts. As for the rest, alcoholism is a disease and you've come so far. Why are you telling me this now?'

Her mum looked uncomfortable for the first time since she'd arrived. 'Because I made a mess of my life and I don't want you to do the same.'

Maya frowned, having no idea where this was going. A big part of her was thrilled that she was actually having a long lucid conversation with her mum, the kind of conversation she wished she could've had over the last few months following Joe's death and the ensuing dramas with Riley.

'I'm fine, Mum.'

'I saw your picture in a magazine, kissing a man,' her mum blurted out, releasing Maya's hand and fiddling with the ring binding on her notebook.

'That was nothing,' Maya said quickly, hoping she didn't blush. The memory of that scorching impulsive kiss with Riley had been replayed numerous times, usually in the wee small hours of the mornings when she lay awake, sad, lonely, wishing things were different.

Her mum chuckled. 'If that was nothing, wish I'd had more of it in my day. Is he special? He must be for you to go around kissing him so soon after the other one died.'

Maya smiled at her mum's derogatory reference to Joe. She'd introduced them on another of her mum's good days and Jill had hated Joe on sight, visibly recoiling from him at one stage. The feeling had been entirely mutual.

'He's a friend, nothing more.'

Though that was a lie. After Riley had left last night, she doubted he'd ever come knocking again in a friendly capacity or otherwise. It was the 'otherwise' that kept her up at nights, fantasising about how good it could be if he was anyone but Joe's brother.

'The article said he was the other one's brother.'

Great. Her mum had just about echoed her thoughts.

'Yes, Riley is Joe's brother.'

'And?'

Maya sighed, choosing her words carefully. She didn't want to talk about her feelings for Riley and the uselessness of her situation and she sure didn't need her mum dishing out agony aunt advice.

'Riley has helped me out a fair bit. He's a good man.'

Her mum nodded, apparently satisfied. 'Thought so. Handsome devil too by that photo. If I'd had a man like him, I would've hung on to him for grim death. Instead, I botched things up by choosing a loser and, rather than moving on afterwards, I wasted my life regretting it every day. A stupid, pointless waste of time when I could've found a better man and had a better life for myself and for you. You were practically a baby when your father left and I could've found a good man, given you a proper family of your own.'

Her mum suddenly sat bolt upright, stuffed the notebook back between the cushions and grabbed both of Maya's hands, gripping tightly. 'That is why I told you about your father. The other one reminded me of him the minute I laid eyes on him. Scum of the earth, his type, despite the fancy clothes and crocodile smile and false charms. You could've done so much better but what could I say? Why would you have listened to me? But I can say this now: if there is anything behind that kiss, any feeling at all, you hang on to this man. Good ones like him don't come along every day and you deserve the best, my darling girl. Something I could never give you.'

'Oh, Mum.' Maya fell into her mother's arms, hugging her like she'd never hugged her before.

In fact they'd rarely touched at all their entire lives, both women flinching away from human contact.

Her mum pulled away first, gently wiping the dampness from Maya's cheeks. 'You know what's in your heart, darling. Follow it. Do the right thing.'

'I can't,' Maya whispered, while a tiny spark of hope flared to life deep in her soul, whispering back, *But what if you can?*

CHAPTER FOURTEEN

RILEY SIPPED AT his Scotch and grimaced, hating the kick-in-your-gut taste but needing something strong to fortify his nerves for the confrontation with Maya.

For that was what it was—a confrontation, not a meeting. Her tone during their brief phone call had made that more than clear.

It had been three days since his ownership proposal, three long days where he'd finalised countless business deals, tidied up the odd loose end at the office via phone and the Net and visited a travel agent where he'd picked up a stack of brochures. The stupid thing was, he'd only flicked through a few, his mind constantly drawn to Maya.

The Greek islands looked good, but then he'd think of her and Chas beside him frolicking in the too-blue Mediterranean.

Ireland looked good, but then he'd imagine them all touring the Emerald Isle, strolling through the lush countryside during the day and sleeping in quaint little B&Bs at night.

Mauritius, the Maldives, Tahiti—they all looked great for a little time out and then he'd remember Maya's infectious laugh or Chas's cheeky grin and he knew that Melbourne held the greatest appeal by far.

'Hi there.'

Deep in thought, he hadn't heard Maya sneak up on him and he accidentally sloshed Scotch over his trousers at the sound of her voice.

'Hi.'

There he went again, slaying her with scintillating conversation. Just once he'd like to have one tenth of Joe's skill with the ladies. His brother might've had many faults but he could charm the tea cosy off a teapot.

Maya frowned as her gaze strayed from his half empty glass to the spreading stain on his leg and he crossed his legs to hide it while quickly placing the remains of his drink on the small glass table in front of him.

'Thanks for meeting me,' she said, sliding into the chair opposite while he tried not to stare.

For starters, she wore soft beige hipster trousers with a figure-hugging chocolate-brown sleeveless polo, a sassy outfit in total contrast with her usual casual attire.

And, for a woman who never wore make-up, she'd done something to her eyes, making them appear wider and sparkling while a faint pink stained her cheeks and her mouth glistened with some sort of gloss.

Whatever, he needed to focus on the words coming out of that sexy mouth and not his urge to plant his lips firmly on it.

'No problem. After the other night, I didn't think you'd want to see me for a while. A long while.'

He opted for honesty, something he'd always been able to do with her. Except for the bit about how much he wanted to be included in the family package he envisaged for Chas, that was.

She shook her head, tousled blonde curls cascading around her face, making him itch to reach out and twist one around his finger, the way she'd unintentionally twisted him around hers.

'You blew me away with that ownership business, that's for sure. But, like I said, I know you mean well. In fact, I think you've always had our best interests at heart, mine and Chas's. You're that kind of guy. Special.'

'Too right,' he said, a warm glow spreading through him at her praise. If only she meant 'special' in the way he hoped.

'That's actually what I wanted to talk to you about.'

Her genuine smile lifted his spirits higher than they'd been in days and he wondered how he'd survive without seeing her on a daily basis, spending quality time with her and the little guy.

'Sounds intriguing, but how about a drink first?'

And just like that, her smile faded—fast. 'Sure, I'll have the usual,' she said, her lips compressing in that awful line that aged her ten years.

He'd noticed that she never touched alcohol and had attributed her aversion to the way Joe had died. Yet maybe a shot of brandy or something similar would make this conversation easier for her?

'Sure you won't have something stronger than a lime and soda?'

'No.' Short, sharp, cold.

'Okay.' He placed her order quickly and took another fortifying sip of his own drink, trying not to pull a face as the liquid burned a trail down his throat. 'Go ahead, I'm all ears.'

Her eyes narrowed and she waited till he'd placed his drink down, as if assessing him. For what he wasn't sure but the speculative gleam in her eyes made him uncomfortable.

'I visited my mum yesterday.'

'What?'

He jolted forward, momentarily wondering if the few sips he'd had on an empty stomach had affected his faculties. He was sure Maya had just said she had a mother when he'd assumed she was dead from one of their early discussions.

'You didn't know she's alive?'

'No. From what you've said before, I thought you had no family.'

Something in her eyes shifted. Guilt? Pain? 'In a way, I guess I've felt that way for a long time.'

She sipped at the lime and soda that had just been placed in front of her, tracing circles in the condensation on the glass and concentrating on the task as if she were trying to solve a physics equation.

'Where is she?'

He asked the question to bring her back to the present rather than any great need to know the answer. There was obviously a story behind her reticence and he wouldn't push her. He'd tried that with the ownership papers and look how that had turned out.

Maya slowly raised her eyes to meet his, glistening green clashing with confused blue. 'Mum's in a special accommodation home. She's been there for the last three years after it got too much for me to look after her.'

'Is she sick?'

She nodded, pain flickering in the green depths again. 'Yes. She's an alcoholic.'

Riley had been expecting any number of diseases like cancer or Parkinson's or Multiple Sclerosis but the minute she told him several things fell into place at once—her aversion to drinking and her emotional shutdown after Joe's death. Considering his brother's death had been caused by a lethal combination of too much alcohol and speed, it must've torn her apart taking into account what she'd just told him.

'She's recovering?'

'Uh-huh. She's been sober since she went into the home. It's part of their rules. Though in a way, she doesn't have much choice. I pay the bills, she doesn't have spare cash to buy alcohol with and even if she did, her mind wanders most days.'

Maya's bottom lip quivered ever so slightly and he knew things must be a lot worse than she was telling him.

'I'm sorry. It must be tough on both of you.'

'You don't know the half of it,' she murmured, taking several gulps of her drink and blinking rapidly.

'I had a pretty hard childhood which is why I'm so protective of Chas.'

She sighed heavily and leaned back as if she'd said something profound when in fact she hadn't told him much more than he knew already. He'd always thought she was overprotective of the little guy but had put it down to the rough time she'd had with Joe rather than her own childhood.

'He's your child. You have every right to protect him.'

Maya didn't speak, staring into her almost empty glass, swirling the lime wedge with her straw in slow, lazy circles.

'Is that what you wanted to talk to me about? To explain your reasoning behind refusing the apartment?'

Silence. An awkward growing silence which had him shuffling in his seat and wondering what the hell was going on.

He polished off the rest of his drink and all but slammed the glass on the table, anything to get her attention, to get her to say something.

Finally she raised stricken eyes to his and said in a soft voice he barely heard, 'I just wanted you to understand.'

'Understand what?'

'Everything,' she said, sitting bolt upright and sliding her glass on to the table. 'But I can't do this here. I need some air. Walk with me?'

Before he could react, she jumped up and scuttled out on to the Promenade, almost tripping in her haste.

Maya walked quickly, striding past people strolling

along the banks of the Yarra in the gorgeous summer sunshine.

Riley caught up within a few paces and she forced herself to slow down, knowing she needed to finish what she'd come to say but feeling increasingly out of her depth with every second.

She'd hoped to divulge her true feelings and see if he could find it in his kind heart to grow to love her like he loved Chas.

She'd psyched herself up for it, dressing to impress, even wearing make up to boost her lousy self esteem. But the minute she'd walked into the trendy bar-cum-café where they'd met for pre-dinner drinks the night of the Ball, had seen his unsteady hand as he'd spilt his drink and smelt the awful pungent Scotch, her resolve had wavered.

Common sense told her Riley wasn't a drunk but once planted, the seed of doubt in her mind took root. Joe had been obsessed with alcohol, using it as a crutch. What if Riley was the same? He looked like hell. Maybe her turning down his offer to provide a home for Chas had sent him into a spiral and he'd reached for a drink to help him cope?

Stupid, irrational doubts but, once there, they'd been enough to stifle her big tell-all session. Probably for the best, considering he probably thought she was a fruit-cake for her erratic behaviour.

'Maya?'

Riley laid a hand on her shoulder as they reached the footbridge and she stopped, knowing it was time to finish this one way or another.

'This is complicated,' she said, trying to shrug off his hand, which felt way too good resting possessively on her shoulder.

'Fine. I can do complicated. And, by the way, stop trying to wriggle away. I'm not letting go of you ever again,' he said, hanging on to her arm and gently dragging her to a wrought iron bench on the river's edge while she secretly wished he meant that literally. 'Now, sit and tell me exactly what 'this' is all about.'

He didn't sound angry and his face wore its usual patient expression though confusion lit his eyes, a dazzling blue reflection of the clear Melbourne sky overhead.

'This is *this!*' She pointed to his hand resting possessively on hers and their close proximity, thigh to thigh, shoulder to shoulder. She'd attributed her pounding heart to the speed she'd been walking though the minute he'd sat next to her, her pulse rate had sped up rather than slowing. 'You. Me. The time we spend together. The friendship.'

She bit her lip, wanting to say more, terrified to do so.

Thankfully, he read her mind like he always did. 'There's more to 'this', isn't there?'

'Yes! No! Oh, heck.'

He slid his arm around her shoulder and she sagged against him before she realised what she was doing. When she tried to sit up, he held her tighter and she relinquished the last of her reticence and snuggled into him, savouring the solid warmth of his body next to hers and wishing he could hold her like this for ever.

'You are one of the most confusing women I have

ever known. One minute you're freezing me out, the next you're soft and vulnerable and I want to hold you like this for ever.'

Maya's pulse spiked as he echoed her own silent wish of a second ago before realising what he meant. He thought she was vulnerable, just like he always had and in true Riley Bourke fashion he had to save her.

Riley the crusader for the downtrodden, pulling on his superhero cape and rescuing her at the slightest hint of trouble.

Well, she was through with being rescued. She needed more and, if he couldn't give it to her, she'd give him a painful wedgy with that superhero underwear he wore on the outside of his jeans.

'Well, you can't.' She struggled to an upright position and shrugged out of his embrace. 'Forever is a long time and I only want to be held that way by a guy who means it.'

To her annoyance he chuckled—a deep, rich sound which made her want to laugh too.

'A guy who means it? By 'it' I'm assuming you mean 'this'?'

He gently cupped her face and turned her towards him, his blue eyes blazing with desire, a startling passion which took her breath away. She waited as he framed her face with his hands and leaned forwards, his lips inching towards her with maddening slowness.

Probably giving her an out, knowing him, and she closed the remaining distance between them in record time, desperate for his kiss.

Fireworks exploded in her head as his lips moved on hers, teasing, commanding, giving, taking.

A long, hot, open-mouthed kiss which had her wanting to dive into the river to cool off before she did something crazy like strip off and jump him.

The type of kiss she'd dreamed of since she'd acknowledged her forbidden feelings for him, the type of kiss which would seal her fate once and for all.

After a mind-blowing, toe-curling eternity, he broke the kiss, his thumbs tracing her lips, which felt as if they'd swelled to double their size. Could be a reaction to the new lip gloss she'd tried for the first time? Nah…

'I'm hoping 'it' was to your satisfaction.'

She whacked him on the arm, trying to look serious and failing miserably. It was difficult to remain aloof when she'd just been thoroughly kissed by the man of her dreams.

'*This* was never meant to happen,' she said, turning her head slightly to plant a soft kiss in the palm of his hand before taking both his hands in hers.

He nodded, his face falling. 'Because of your love for Joe.'

'Is that what you think?'

'Of course. What other reason could there be?'

Maya shook her head and glanced around, watching a canoe float by, business people scurrying along and the odd couple holding hands while taking a leisurely stroll along the river.

She wanted to be one of those romantic couples. She

yearned for it. And there was only one way she would get it. By telling the truth. All of it.

'I don't love Joe. I'm not sure if I ever loved Joe.'

Riley frowned, an adorable indentation between his brows, and she resisted the urge to lean over and smooth it away with a reassuring kiss. 'But I thought—'

'Wrong. Joe swept me off my feet and made me forget my problems. He made me fall in love with him out of sheer persistence and I fell quickly. I'd never been with a guy before; I'd been looking after my mum full time while juggling a job at the stables and I didn't have a social life let alone a suave guy like Joe to look twice at me. It went to my head.'

Riley didn't interrupt. He merely squeezed her hands as if urging her to continue.

'And addled my brains. I was so besotted with the idea of being in love rather than the guy I was supposed to be in love with that I went along for the ride. Then I moved in with him, I got pregnant, he proposed and things went downhill from there.'

'You looked so happy that first night, like the perfect couple.'

'Joe wanted it to look that way. He had a habit of charming me one minute, treating me like a dog the next. I stuck around for the sake of our unborn baby and I tried to make it work, hoping that after the birth things would improve. They didn't and when he started drinking and playing around, any residual feelings I had died.'

'I wish I'd known,' Riley said, his mouth turned down in sadness, the frown deepening.

'It wouldn't have changed anything. I tried hard to make it work to provide Chas with a stable home environment. I guess I hoped that marriage would change Joe.'

She took a deep breath, knowing her next words were mortifying but knowing she had to tell Riley everything if he were to understand. 'The more I pushed, the angrier he grew till we had a huge argument the night he died. After he came back from being out with you. The night he told me the real reason why he'd courted me in the first place.'

Riley placed a finger against her lips. 'Shh. You don't have to tell me. I know.'

'You know?'

He nodded, anger tightening his handsome features. 'Joe had this stupid hang-up his entire life, always trying to compete with me, trying to beat me at everything. He never did and I guess it just drove him to do crazy things. He craved everything I wanted and when he saw the way I looked at you at the Ball, he went for it. It was just a stupid game to him, a way to make me sweat, taking away a woman I was interested in.'

Maya's heart flip-flopped. Riley had been interested in her that first night? But, if that were true, everything that had happened in the last few months between them took on a new light.

Maybe the time he had spent with them hadn't just been about Chas? And maybe, just maybe, he felt the connection between them and, dared she say it, the love that filled her heart?

She leaned forward and placed a soft lingering kiss

on his lips, emboldened by the knowledge that a man like him could've wanted a girl like her.

'You were interested in me? Really?'

'Really,' he murmured against her lips, grazing them repeatedly with his own. 'I remember we did the whole eye contact thing and I smiled at you and then Joe stepped into the picture.'

She flushed with joy, pulling away reluctantly, needing to finish her story. 'And I picked Joe over you. No accounting for taste, is there?'

Her laugh sounded forced, brittle, and he traced a slow sensuous trail down her cheek with his lips.

She closed her eyes, savouring his caress, wishing it could go on for ever. But she had to tell him the whole truth if they were to have any chance. Opening her eyes, she pulled away gently and placed a finger on his lips to hush him. 'There's more. The reason Joe gave you wasn't the only one and, until now, I had no idea about his competing with you.'

'You didn't?'

Confusion clouded Riley's startling blue eyes and she almost wished she didn't have to tell him the rest, which she hoped wouldn't turn the confusion to disbelief.

'No, that wasn't the reason Joe gave me. In a way, I wish it was.'

She glanced away, lost in the memory of that fateful night when Joe had battered her minuscule self-esteem to an all-time low and how she'd reacted. By insulting his manhood, by saying she'd never loved him and if he was half the man his brother was, she might feel something other than loathing for him. She hadn't known Riley then but his convenient appearance that night and Joe's nonsensical accusation that she liked him had made her compare Joe to his brother. She'd wanted to hurt him as much as he'd hurt her.

The result? He'd stormed out and wrapped himself around a pole, leaving her with a gnawing guilt that she'd carried upon her shoulders, preventing her from moving on, from being happy.

Thankfully, the time had come to shrug off the weight and take a chance on the love she'd been searching for her entire life.

Taking a deep breath, she looked Riley straight in the eye.

'Joe told me the only reason he'd looked twice at a scruffy tomboy like me was because he wanted inside information from the track for his gambling. 'Straight from the horse's mouth', were his exact words. As you probably know, courtesy of his bankrupt status, he had major debts and desperately needed cash. He couldn't stop gambling and thought the only way to break his losing streak and become a winner was to hook up with me. I worked on the inside and he wanted to know it all. I gave him nothing, which is why he took his plan to the next level, convincing me to move in with him. However, he hadn't planned on the pregnancy, which threw a major spanner in his scheme. He wanted enough tips to earn the cash to clear his debts, then I was out of there. The pregnancy forced his hand and, though he proposed to make it look good for everyone else, particularly the media he adored, the minute I fell pregnant was the minute he started really hating me.'

'Oh, my God,' Riley murmured, gripping her hands tightly in his, shock streaked across his face. 'I can't believe Joe put you through that.'

'Believe it,' she said softly, feeling the first fluttering of relief at unburdening herself and wanting to go the whole way. 'He tried to make me have a termination and I knew then that the man I'd fallen for wasn't the prince I'd first thought. However, he was the first guy in my life to give me what I thought was love, to pay some attention to me. I never knew my father and wanted a family of my own more than anything so I decided to make the best of it. However, my best wasn't good enough and when Chas was born, our relationship continued to spiral downhill with Joe's increased drinking and absences. You know the rest.'

Anger blazed from his eyes, swiftly replaced by tenderness as tears pricked her eyelids. 'You know what I know? That my brother was a fool. An absolute total ass, a selfish little boy inside a grown man's body who had no thought for anyone but himself. He didn't deserve a woman like you and, if he were here today, I'd beat the living daylights out of him for what he put you through.'

'My hero to the end,' she said, smiling through her tears, eternally grateful that he hadn't clammed up or run a mile after hearing her pathetic story. She'd never intended on playing the victim but hearing her story out loud painted her in that light and she didn't like it. She never had, which was why she needed to take control of her life, starting this very minute.

'Can I ask you something?'

He nodded, his compassionate expression encouraging her to continue down the path of no return. 'Anything.'

She looked up at him from beneath lowered lashes, an unconscious flirty action which made her feel the teensiest bit naughty. 'You said you were interested in me earlier. Interested as in past tense?'

The corners of his delicious mouth twitched and she itched to lean over and give him a good reason to smile, like another scorching kiss.

'I'm interested all right. I want you, Maya Edison. Want, as in present tense, as in the last few months with you have been the happiest of my life. Want, as in I'm in love with you and haven't got the foggiest idea what to do about it as everything I try ends in disaster. Want, as in I want us to be a family—you, me and that delightful little man of yours. Want, as in I want it all. With you.'

His lips never had the chance to make it into a full-blown smile as she launched herself at him, straddling his lap, wrapping her arms tightly around him and kissing him with every ounce of love she had pent up for this amazing guy.

Riley loved her.

He *loved* her!

She should've known. Even without saying the words, he'd demonstrated his feelings in so many ways so many times.

Her hero in every way.

Chuckling softly as they came up for air, he said, 'So what do you want? Apart from my body, that is.'

She laughed, a loud joyous sound which came straight from the heart and she didn't care when people turned to stare.

Let them. She was through with gossip and innuendo and lies. The truth that Riley loved her and she loved him was all that mattered.

Their love would protect Chas from any potential scandal because by the time he was old enough to understand they would be a happily married couple celebrating their umpteenth anniversary.

'You really want to know what I want?'

Her heart pounded with the desire simmering in his eyes, a desire she could feel with her legs wrapped around his waist. A desire which thrilled her, aroused her and empowered her like nothing else ever had. A man like Riley Bourke wanted her, loved her, giving her self esteem the boost it needed.

'Yeah, I really want to know.' He shifted against her, his smile turning wicked in an instant.

'I want a family of my own. You, me and Chas. For ever. I want to have your babies. I want us to grow old together. I want *you*.'

She wriggled closer—if that were even possible—and poured every ounce of what she was feeling into her words. 'I love you, Riley. I love everything about you, from your kind heart to your generosity and compassion for others. But, most of all, I love how you love me. And how you love Chas. You're one in a million'

His hands caressed her back, sending heat shimmering through her body. 'Wow. That's some testimonial. You sure? Most times we were together I didn't even think you liked me all that much.'

She grinned and tweaked his nose. 'Didn't you ever have a girl in primary school tease you, ignore you and break all your pencils?'

'Can't remember back that far,' he said with a grimace. 'I'm ten years older than you.'

Maya rolled her eyes. 'I bet you did and that meant the girl liked you. Guess I was doing the same thing unconsciously. You know, being horrible when I liked you all along.'

'Loved me, you mean,' he growled, burying his face in her neck and snuggling till she giggled.

'Speaking of love, you know we're getting married, right?'

His head snapped up at that and, by the stunned, ecstatic expression spreading across his face, she had her answer before he opened his mouth.

'Right,' he said, tipping her chin up to gaze into her eyes. 'Now, how about we make up for lost time with more of that kissing you're so good at?'

'I like the way you think.'

Maya liked the way he kissed even more.

EPILOGUE

'GO, GIRL, GO!'

Maya shifted from side to side, leaning as far forward on the rails as she could with her eight-month pregnant belly, trying to get a glimpse of the horses as they rounded the final turn.

'She's hit the front,' Riley said, clasping her hand tightly while trying to constrain an exuberant Chas with the other. 'She's going to win.'

'I can't take any more excitement.'

Maya closed her eyes, letting the sound of people cheering and horses pounding up the straight wash over her. She missed this: being part of the action, the thrill of winning, surrounded by friends and colleagues who cared.

Those same friends and colleagues who had attended her small, intimate wedding to Riley nine months earlier at this very same venue, though Flemington had been a lot quieter that day, unless she counted Chas's whining to go for a horsie ride all through the reception brunch and her sobbing when it came time to exchange the final vows.

'Mum, Dad, horsie win. Horsie win!' Chas yelled and Maya opened her eyes in time to see Material Girl flash past the finishing post to win her second Melbourne Cup in succession.

'Yay! Yay!' Chas clapped his hands excitedly, Riley enveloped them in a group hug and Maya battled tears as sheer unadulterated joy swept through her.

'She won,' Maya murmured, her tear-filled gaze locking on Riley's tender one.

'We're all winners, my love,' he said, slanting a slow burning kiss across her lips, the type of kiss that Maya loved and savoured and treasured every day she was lucky enough to have with this incredible man.

'We sure are.'

She smiled at her husband, her son and caressed her swollen belly.

Winners were grinners and, with a family like theirs, she would never stop smiling.

* * * * *

Next month in
THE NANNY AND THE SHEIKH (#3928),
Barbara McMahon sweeps you away
to the exotic kingdom of Qu'Arim
in the next installment of
THE BRIDES OF BELLA LUCIA.

Years ago Sheikh Surim Al-Thani was called back to his kingdom Qu'Arim following the sudden death of his father. He determined to be a mature and responsible ruler, dedicated to his people. But when his cousin's three children were tragically orphaned, they came to the palace to be raised by the sheikh. Surim had no idea how to deal with the children or their grief. But now a chance encounter with professional nanny Melissa Fox offers a temporary solution… But can she heal the heart of the sheikh?

Sunday morning, Max and Melissa caught an early flight to Rome where they changed for a plane to Qu'Arim. It was late afternoon when they landed. Immediately after exiting the plane, Melissa raised her face to the sun. Its warmth felt fabulous! The air was perfumed with the sweet scent of plumeria mixed with that of airplane fuel. The soft breeze that wafted across her skin felt as silky as down. Soon they'd be away from the airport and she could really enjoy scents that vied for identification.

"I already love it here," she said as they walked across the tarmac.

"Did you say something?" Max asked, a bit distracted. He was in full business mode, having worked on the plane and now carrying his briefcase almost as if it were a part of him. Melissa wasn't surprised. The man loved his work. He ate, slept and breathed it as far as she could tell. Though he wasn't a hermit. He did his fair share of dating, according to her mother.

"It's nice here," she said, trying to match his businesslike attitude. Inside, however, she felt sheer excitement. She hoped she had some free time to explore while she was here. And maybe spend an afternoon at the beach. The Persian Gulf had been a heavenly blue when they had circled preparing to land.

They were met inside the terminal by a tall man with dark hair and almost black eyes. He smiled at Max when he spotted him and Melissa felt her heart skip a beat. She'd thought Max handsome, but this guy was something else! His charcoal-gray suit and red power tie were very western. She glanced around; most of the men wore suits, few wore the more traditional Arab robes.

In fact, she could have been in any airport in Europe. For a moment she was disappointed. She wanted to see more the exotic aspects of this country, not find it was just like any other capital she'd seen.

Melissa spotted two men standing nearby, scanning the crowd. The local equivalent of guards, she guessed from the way they behaved.

Max turned and made the introductions. Sheikh Surim Al-Thani inclined his head slightly, reaching for Melissa's hand and bringing it to his lips. The warmth of his lips startled her, but it was the compelling gaze in those dark eyes that mesmerized. She felt her heart race, heat flooded through her and she wondered if he came with a warning label—dangerous to a woman's equilibrium.

"Welcome to Qu'Arim," he said formally, his voice deep and smooth with the faintest hint of accent. "I hope your stay will be enjoyable. Please let me know if there is anything I can provide for you while you are here."

"Thank you," Melissa mumbled, feeling halfway infatuated by the sheer animal magnetism she sensed in the man. She could listen to him all day. His hand was warm and firm, almost seeming to caress before he released hers. She felt a fluttering of awareness at his intensity when he looked at her. Giving herself a mental shake, she tried to think of the mundane reason for her visit. She was definitely not here to get a crush on Max's friend.

She glanced back and forth between the two men as they spoke. Both carried an air of assurance and confidence that was as appealing as their looks. But it was Surim who captured her attention. Before she could think about it further, their host gestured toward the entrance.

Their small group began to move toward the front of the airport. She gladly let Max and Surim talk together while she looked eagerly around, taking in the crowds of travelers in the various dress. There was a mixture of languages, some she recognized as European. She wondered how hard it would be to learn some Arabic while she was here.

Melissa and Max were ushered into a luxurious stretch limousine while one of the men attending the sheikh went to fetch their luggage. Melissa settled back in her seat and gazed at the landscape, trying to ignore the growing sense of awareness she felt around the sheikh. He joined them after speaking to his men and Melissa was hard pressed not to stare. Resolutely she gazed out the window.

Flowers and soaring palms lined the avenue, softening the austere lines of the airport terminal.

As the sheikh continued his discussion with Max as the limo pulled away from the airport she occasionally glanced in his direction, intrigued as never before. Surim Al-Thani was slightly shorter than Max, but at six feet still towered over her own five feet three inches. His dark hair gleamed. She wondered if it was as thick and silky as it looked.

When he met her gaze she felt flustered. She had been rude. Yet when his eyes caught hers for an instant she continued boldly staring—this time directly into his dark gaze. Growing uncomfortably warm, Melissa finally broke contact and again looked out the side window. Her heart skipped a beat, then pounded gently in her chest.

Let *Margaret Way* enchant you with
these tales from the outback.

Introducing

Outback Marriages

these bush bachelors are looking for a bride!

Outback Man Seeks Wife

BY MARGARET WAY

On sale January 2007

---

*Cattle Rancher,
Convenient Wife*

BY MARGARET WAY

On sale March 2007

nocturne™

**WAS HE HER SAVIOR
OR HER NIGHTMARE?**

HAUNTED
LISA CHILDS

Years ago, Ariel and her sisters were separated for
their own protection. Now the man who vowed
revenge on her family has resumed the hunt, and
Ariel must warn her sisters before it's too late.
The closer she comes to finding them, the more
secretive her fiancé becomes. Can she trust the man
she plans to spend eternity with? Or has he been
waiting for the perfect moment to destroy her?

On sale December 2006.

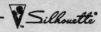

SPECIAL EDITION™

Silhouette Special Edition brings you a heartwarming new story from the *New York Times* bestselling author of *McKettrick's Choice*

LINDA LAEL MILLER

Sierra's Homecoming

Sierra's Homecoming follows the parallel lives of two McKettrick women, living their lives in the same house but generations apart, each with a special son and an unlikely new romance.

December 2006

REQUEST YOUR FREE BOOKS!
2 FREE NOVELS PLUS 2
FREE GIFTS!

HARLEQUIN ROMANCE®

From the Heart, For the Heart

YES! Please send me 2 FREE Harlequin Romance® novels and my 2 FREE gifts. After receiving them, if I don't wish to receive any more books, I can return the shipping statement marked "cancel." If I don't cancel, I will receive 4 brand-new novels every month and be billed just $3.57 per book in the U.S., or $4.05 per book in Canada, plus 25¢ shipping and handling per book and applicable taxes, if any*. That's a savings of over 15% off the cover price! I understand that accepting the 2 free books and gifts places me under no obligation to buy anything. I can always return a shipment and cancel at any time. Even if I never buy another book from Harlequin, the two free books and gifts are mine to keep forever.

114 HDN EEV7   314 HDN EEWK

Name	(PLEASE PRINT)	
Address		Apt.
City	State/Prov.	Zip/Postal Code

Signature (If under 18, a parent or guardian must sign)

Mail to Harlequin Reader Service®:

IN U.S.A.
P.O. Box 1867
Buffalo, NY
14240-1867

IN CANADA
P.O. Box 609
Fort Erie, Ontario
L2A 5X3

Not valid to current Harlequin Romance subscribers.

Want to try two free books from another line?

Call 1-800-873-8635 or visit www.morefreebooks.com.

* Terms and prices subject to change without notice. NY residents add applicable sales tax. Canadian residents will be charged applicable provincial taxes and GST. This offer is limited to one order per household. All orders subject to approval. Credit or debit balances in a customer's account(s) may be offset by any other outstanding balance owed by or to the customer. Please allow 4 to 6 weeks for delivery.

HR06

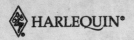

Coming Next Month

#3927 OUTBACK MAN SEEKS WIFE Margaret Way
Outback Marriages

Returning to his dilapidated ranch, Clay Cunningham intends to settle down and find himself a wife. Local-girl Caroline McNevin is as fragile and innocent as Clay is proud and rugged. Something in her vulnerability touches Clay, but first Caroline needs to confront her past.

#3928 THE NANNY AND THE SHEIKH Barbara McMahon
The Brides of Bella Lucia

Melissa Fox's trip to the kingdom of Qu'Arim is a perk of her job at Bella Lucia. When she expertly calms Sheikh Surim Al-Thani's three little children, he is determined she will stay on as his nanny. Soon she finds herself falling for a man she could only ever dream of marrying.

#3929 THE BUSINESSMAN'S BRIDE Jackie Braun

Art photographer Anne Lundy was proud of her independence. But when she needed help from straitlaced family-friend Richard Danton, Anne found herself unexpectedly attracted to him—and eager to find out what would happen if he lost control.

#3930 MEANT-TO-BE MOTHER Ally Blake

Single-father James Dillon has dedicated his life to his young son. Yet when a beautiful stranger appears on his doorstep, he can't ignore the magnetism between them. Siena Capuletti didn't mean to fall in love; can she overcome the mistakes of the past for the sake of James and his adorable son?